JANIE BOLITHO was born in Falmouth, Cornwall. She enjoyed a variety of careers – psychiatric nurse, debt collector, working for a tour operator, a book-maker's clerk – before becoming a full-time writer. She passed away in 2002.

By Janie Bolitho

Snapped in Cornwall
Framed in Cornwall
Buried in Cornwall
Betrayed in Cornwall
Plotted in Cornwall
Killed in Cornwall
Caught Out in Cornwall

BETRAYED IN CORNWALL

JANIE BOLITHO

Allison & Busby Limited
12 Fitzroy Mews
London W1T 6DW
allisonandbusby.com

First published in Great Britain in 2000.
This paperback edition published by Allison & Busby in 2015.

A CIP catalogue record for this book is available from
the British Library.

10 9 8 7 6 5 4 3 2

ISBN 978-0-7490-1789-7

Typeset in 10.5/15.5 pt Sabon by
Allison & Busby Ltd.

The paper used for this Allison & Busby publication
has been produced from trees that have been legally sourced
from well-managed and credibly certified forests.

Printed and bound by
CPI Group (UK) Ltd, Croydon, CR0 4YY

For Isobel Amy Bolitho, my grand-daughter

CHAPTER ONE

For three weeks the sun had shone relentlessly. June could be wet and windy, but not that year. Still, Rose Trevelyan thought, we had our share of rain in May; torrential rain, day after day of heavy showers and strong winds which had flung the sea shorewards, up over the Promenade in Penzance, over the pebbles in Newlyn and up as far as the Green. Even now the grass was verdant with no sign of yellowing. And no sign of cutting either, Rose admonished herself, staring at the lumpy lawn at the side of the house, a pencil held to her lips.

Her paintings were ready for her first solo exhibition. She had spent the day in her studio, working on the job she so disliked, and had framed them herself. Geoff Carter, who owned a gallery in Penzance and had offered her the exhibition, had suggested several excellent framers in the area but Rose had insisted the work should be all her own. '"Vanity, like murder, will out,"' she quoted, aware that she wanted all the credit to be hers. She frowned. A single line bisected her high forehead. Where was the quotation from and why had she remembered it? 'Damn. I'll have to look it up.'

Before she could do so the telephone rang. It was Etta Chynoweth, a widow like herself, asking if she fancied a walk.

'There's nothing I'd like more. I've been cooped up inside all day. Shall I meet you by the Newlyn Art Gallery in, say, twenty minutes?' Rose hung up, glanced at the cloudless sky and decided she did not need a jacket. For once, her clothes were not splattered with paint. The tight-fitting jeans, plain lemon T-shirt and rope-soled sneakers were smart enough should they decide to stop for a drink. And she had the feeling that they might do so, that Etta needed someone in whom to confide.

Having locked the kitchen door which led to the steeply sloping garden at the side of the house, Rose walked down the path to the road which wound downhill all the way to her destination.

Outside the Star Inn two fishermen she knew were talking. They waved and smiled and, once she had passed, one of them whistled. Rose blushed appreciatively but did not turn around. Although she was nearing fifty, from behind she might have been twenty. Her wavy auburn hair was held in a velvet clip at the nape of her neck and the few strands of grey were barely visible. Even full face she looked nowhere near her age.

The gallery was on the edge of Newlyn, right on the seafront, and was backed by a long stretch of grass where children were playing, shouting to one another as they kicked a ball about or rode their bikes. Rose could hear their cries before she saw them.

She rounded the corner where the high wall protected the cottages in Tolcarne Terrace from the winter onslaught of the sea and paused. Dog walkers were on the only part of the beach where their pets were allowed in the summer. Most areas were prohibited between Easter and October. Each day the view of the wide sweep of the bay differed depending on the tide and the weather. The tide was in now, the water as smooth as a sheet of cellophane. It lapped imperceptibly at the rocks beneath the sea wall and gave off a clean salty scent. On its surface a noisy flock of black-headed gulls squabbled, the chocolate brown hood of their summer plumage in stark contrast to their white feathers and red bills. Rose watched them, smiling at their spitefulness. They were far noisier and more vicious than the larger herring-gull. To her artist's eye they formed a good picture, their colouring enhanced by the limpid milky-green water. She turned and saw Etta approaching. She wore a smart cotton dress but looked tired and drawn.

The women were the same age and had both lost their husbands yet they had little else in common, other than friendship.

'Thanks for coming, Rose.' Etta smiled.

'I needed some air, I've spent the day in the attic.' The attic, which she grandly called her studio on occasions, had once been where Rose developed and printed the photographs she took professionally and where she put the final touches to the watercolours she painted. Now she was working in oils, painting as she had always wanted to paint, but she had not relinquished her other work totally – she wasn't quite confident enough to do that yet.

They walked in silence in the direction of Penzance. Words would come later. For now Rose and Etta were content to be out of doors, breathing in the clean air and feeling the sun on their faces.

Rose knew Etta's history. At seventeen she had met a French fisherman whose boat had come into Newlyn harbour. He had left after three days without ever knowing he was later to become a father. 'I was young and naive,' Etta had once told Rose, 'but I don't regret it for one moment. Joe was everything to me until I met Ed.' Later, when Joe was five, she had met and married a steady, reliable electrician called Ed. He had taken the boy on as his own son and he and Etta had then produced Sarah. Ed had died of a coronary thrombosis when he was only forty-three but had left his wife in a comfortable position and in possession of a four-bedroom house facing the bay on the side of a hill. For the past few years she had been doing bed and breakfast.

'You look tired, Etta,' Rose said, glancing sideways at her strong-boned face.

'I am. I haven't been sleeping well and it's been really busy for so early in the season.' She sighed. 'And there's Sarah.'

'Sarah? Is she ill?'

Etta shook her head. 'Not that I know of. She refuses to talk to me. I'm terrified she's on drugs and I don't know what to do about it. And please don't suggest I go and see a counsellor or something. Whatever it is, I want to sort it out myself if I can.'

'Why don't you just ask her outright? You know her well enough to tell if she's lying.'

They had stopped to watch a cormorant skimming the water as it crossed the bay. Occasionally a seal would appear, quite close to the shore, but not that night. 'Now you've said it, it sounds like such a simple solution. But I don't want to alienate her further. It's more than just her age, I'm sure of it.'

'Etta, she's seventeen, the same age as you were when you had Joe. Perhaps she's in love.' Rose laughed. 'Do you remember what it was like at that age? All that anguish, all that posturing and game playing. I'd hate to go through that again.'

'Yes.' Etta looked away and hesitated before saying, 'So would I. Anyway, Joe'll be back tomorrow. I'm always okay when he's around. He's so – well, he's so normal.' Etta laughed. 'You know what I mean. He's a man now, whereas Sarah is a teenage monster. It'll pass, but I wish it would do so quickly.'

'Would you like me to speak to her just in case there is something troubling her? We've always got on well.' Rose bit her lip. Why did I say that? she thought. Why can't I keep my big mouth shut? Interfering had got her into trouble before. At least, so her friends told her. Rose thought of it as curiosity, as a natural desire to help people she cared for.

'Would you? You've no idea how grateful I'd be. She's

more likely to confide in someone outside the family.' Rose Trevelyan was sensible and wise and had the ability to laugh at herself. If only Sarah, who took herself so seriously, could be more like Rose, Etta thought, she might be able to get through to her daughter.

'Leave it to me.' What have I let myself in for now? Rose wondered as they continued in the direction of Penzance. But it must have been hard for Etta, bringing up two children without their respective fathers. Sarah had only been five when Ed died.

'She used to be such a happy little girl. I can't understand the change in her. Sorry, Rose, you don't want to listen to me moaning.'

'That's what friends are for. Now, where shall we have that drink?'

They walked as far as the Yacht, a large 1930s pub set back from the seafront behind St Anthony's Gardens. It was warm enough to sit on one of the slatted wooden seats in front from where they could watch the activity in the bay.

Over the murmur of traffic they discussed Rose's exhibition. Etta said how much she was looking forward to it.

'Bring Sarah, if she'll come,' Rose said. 'You never know, she might enjoy it.' Never having had children of her own Rose was still aware that if Sarah did enjoy it she would show no sign of having done so. Throughout the generations teenagers behaved in that manner; adults accused them of being sullen, their contemporaries thought they were cool. Do they still use that word? Rose wondered.

As they talked Rose thought about Joe. He had the

swarthy complexion of a fisherman and the dark, rugged looks of a Cornishman, yet his mother was fair. He obviously took after his father. Rose liked him without reservation. Joe Chynoweth was open and honest and hard-working and treated his mother with respect because he loved and admired her.

'Rose,' he had said in answer to her question over a glass of beer one Sunday lunchtime when she had invited the family to eat with her, 'they told me at school I could have gone on to further education but I always knew I'd be a fisherman. Maybe it's in the blood. You couldn't work with better people than Jan and Billy and Trevor and I love those lone watches.

'It's hard to describe the summer nights when the sea whispers to you and nudges the boat, when the moonlight ripples on the water and the stars appear far closer than they ever do on land. It gives a man a chance to think.

'I know the outlook isn't great for us, but how could any man sit behind a desk all day without breathing fresh air and feeling the wind on his face? Now that is what I call a hard life.'

Rose had never heard him make such a long speech. 'Yes, but how's the cooking these days?' she had asked with a smile, aware that aboard the trawler all chores were shared and that Joe's efforts in the galley, despite the quantity and quality of the raw ingredients provided, were a cause of mirth to the rest of the crew.

'I'm getting there. I usually manage not to burn one item. This beer's good,' he had added. Rose knew then the cause of his loquacity. Trevor Penfold, one of the crew and the husband of Rose's best friend, had brewed it himself. He had warned her it had a kick.

But despite what Joe had said there was a down side to fishing. There were days when the boat would be tossed on a seemingly empty sea when no other vessel was in sight, when it pitched and rolled in a high swell, when waves crashed over the bows soaking the crew even beneath their oilskins, when nothing was more welcome than St Clement's Island as they entered the bay knowing that the safety of Newlyn harbour was within reach . . .

'Is Joe still seeing Sue Veal?' Rose asked Etta.

'Yes. It's almost a year now. I think they're thinking about getting married.'

'Has he asked her?' Rose placed her empty glass on the wrought-iron table and reached for her cigarettes. 'I don't know. Do people still do that?'

'Probably – at least, people like Joe.'

When Etta laughed her features altered. She was a neat, plain woman but her face had character. Her smile added interest, made her become the sort of person you wanted to get to know. 'Yes. They're both a bit old-fashioned. Him and Sue still living at home. You're right, it wouldn't surprise me if he asks her father's permission. Shall we have another?'

Rose nodded and watched a tourist trying to reverse his car into too small a space. Through the side window she saw his mouth working and guessed what sort of language was issuing from it. Red-faced he changed gear, stepped on the accelerator and shot out into the road with a screech of tyres.

'Look at that,' Rose said when Etta returned carrying two glasses.

To their right the sun was setting. Only half of it was visible as it sank behind the houses of Newlyn casting a pink glow over everything. The turquoise sea had darkened; it was almost purple as the plain bulbs strung between the lamp posts along the Promenade came on in fits and starts.

Behind them the bright lights of the pub spilt out over tables and turned the foliage of the flowers in the tubs along the low wall navy blue. Laughter and cigar smoke were carried towards them in the gentle breeze which heralded the end of the day.

They finished their drinks and walked home slowly, Etta turning off once they'd passed the boating lake on the opposite side of the road from the Promenade. 'I won't forget to speak to Sarah,' Rose called out.

Etta turned to wave. Her face and hair mingled into a white blur in the darkness. 'Thanks, Rose.'

Two more days, Rose thought with excitement as she continued on her way. And my parents will be here to see my exhibition. She did not think she could be happier, unless she could have David back. How proud he would have been. But David had died of cancer. Mostly now her memories were of the good times and she could think of him with deep regret but without the agonising pain she had endured initially.

Her legs began to ache as she took the hill in long strides. She reached the bottom of her drive and saw the faint light shining through the front window. The one in the hall had been set on a time-switch. It was a welcome sight.

Inside, surrounded by things so familiar, things she had never taken for granted, she thought how lucky she was. The two-bedroom house was the one she had lived in throughout the twenty years of her happy marriage and one, she suspected, she would never leave. Stone built, the rooms were small but it was cosy and warm in the winter and cool in the summer. The chintz of the armchairs might be wearing thin but this was of little importance compared with the view. The whole of Mount's Bay was visible, right around to the Lizard Point on a clear day. To Rose it was home and always would be.

It was late, but Rose wasn't tired. She went to the fridge and took out a bottle of Frascati she had opened the previous night and poured herself a glass. She carried it through to the sitting room and sat by the window, which she had opened, and breathed in the smell of lavender which grew outside. There was the summer to look forward to. Rose smiled. 'And autumn and the winter,' she said, unsure which of the seasons she liked best. 'And tomorrow my parents will be here.' How good it would be to see them again.

She finished the wine, closed the window and went up the creaking wooden staircase to bed.

She was physically tired now but excitement kept her awake for some time. Trying not to think that her exhibition might be a flop, she turned her mind to Etta. How awful if Sarah was on drugs. It happened, and too frequently, amongst teenagers. At least Joe would be landing tomorrow; he would take Etta's mind off her problems and he might even be able to talk some sense into his sister. But something other than Sarah was bothering her friend. Etta had seemed – not quite shifty, but as if her mind was elsewhere. In fact, she had been distracted for some time now. I'll speak to Sarah at the first opportunity, Rose decided as her eyelids fluttered and tiredness overcame her.

CHAPTER TWO

Etta's house, like many others, was perched on the side of a hill. The front upstairs rooms overlooked the roofs of the properties below, affording a view of the sea. Seven years previously she had had the attic converted into a bedroom. It was now where Joe slept, leaving two rooms free for guests.

Breakfast was over. Although the windows and the back door were open the air was too still and oppressive to disperse the smell of bacon and sausages which lingered in the kitchen. Etta stepped out on to the paved area where garden furniture and terracotta pots of flowers stood. In her arms was a plastic basket containing wet towels. Sheets and pillowcases churned in the washing machine. She mounted the three concrete steps leading up to the ground which had been levelled and grassed by Ed. Tall flowering shrubs bordered the lawn and provided privacy. In its centre stood two Cornish palms. Their fronds, which tapped like rigging on the masts of ships in the lightest of breezes, were totally still and silent, as was the house. Her guests had gone out for the day and Sarah was still in bed. She would surface when there was no more work to be done then disappear without saying where she was going.

I should insist upon knowing, Etta thought as she pegged the towels to the rotary line which was hidden behind the shrubbery. It just seemed too much of an effort. As far as Sarah was concerned, everything she said and did lately was wrong. Joe had never been like that. Deep down she understood that Sarah was flexing her muscles. Neither child nor woman, she both resented and wished to emulate her mother. I hope Rose can sort her out, she thought, turning with a smile when she heard Joe's voice.

He hugged her, keeping his arm around her shoulder as they went into the house.

Sarah stood in the kitchen wearing a short housecoat and an even shorter nightdress. 'Is there any bread?' she asked.

'It's in the bin, where it always is. Please clear up after youself. I have to get some shopping.' How different they are, she thought, as she picked up her purse and car keys.

The term had not officially ended but Sarah had sat her end-of-year exams and only needed to attend school occasionally. One more year and she would be off to university. Maybe then they could become friends again. Maybe then she could sort out her own life.

Rose stood back and folded her arms, satisfied with the oils which were waiting to be collected. It had taken her almost thirty years to achieve her ambition, her own exhibition.

Fate rather than lack of talent had been responsible.

Originally from Gloucestershire, Rose had come to Cornwall after finishing at art college. She had met and married David Trevelyan, a mining engineer, and had lived in Newlyn ever since. After his death she had rebuilt her life and, since that time, encouraged by friends and fellow painters, she had concentrated less and less on watercolours and photography and returned to her favourite medium which was oils.

Geoff Carter had told her that the gallery could cater for sixty guests for the first night's private viewing. Rose had sent out printed invitations but there had been far fewer than sixty. The people she wanted to come were those who were most dear to her. Geoff had suggested it might be an idea to ask some of the influential people in the area but Rose had declined. This was so special to her that buttering up strangers who might be useful would spoil the evening.

That her parents were coming was her greatest pleasure. She had no other family, the other guests were her closest friends. Barry Rowe in particular. She had known him ever since her arrival in Cornwall. He ran a gift shop which specialised in the work of local artists and craftsmen. For many years Rose had painted wild flowers and village scenes which Barry reproduced as greetings cards and notelets.

During her marriage art had become more of a hobby than a career, although she managed to sell her work via Barry and cafes and tea shops which displayed her paintings on their walls. When David died Rose had discovered that she could manage financially but she had needed something to occupy her time and had taken up photography as well.

Barry Rowe, thin, stoop-shouldered, slightly balding

and with glasses which perpetually slipped down his nose, had been in love with Rose since the day they had met. Unmarried himself, he had stood by her through good times and bad, never giving up hope that one day they would be together. Not once had Rose given him any indication that she felt more than friendship for him, but that did not deter him. Perversely, he had liked and admired David Trevelyan and had helped Rose through the terrible months following his death but he had been sick with envy when, five years later and as fully recovered as she would ever be, she had started seeing Jack Pearce, a detective inspector in the Devon and Cornwall police.

Rose had known all this but could not allow Barry to dominate her life, which he had a tendency to do if she was not firm. She supposed she was thinking of him particularly because of the promise that she had made Etta Chynoweth that she would speak to her daughter. 'Leave well alone,' she could hear Barry say, although he would be wasting his breath. But when and how to do it without making it appear too obvious to the girl? Well, problems like that tended to sort themselves out. Rose went downstairs to wait for Geoff Carter.

The water in the bay was now azure beneath the strong sun. The colours were more vibrant, the light so different from anywhere else that numerous artists were drawn to the area. On days such as today Rose felt she might have been looking out of a window somewhere in the southern Mediterranean.

The kitchen door was wide open but no air circulated. The lawn might be patchy and uneven and in need of a cut but the shrubs and flowers survived regardless, thanks to the temperate climate and plentiful rain.

Geoff's van came up the drive and stopped behind her Metro. It was specially designed to carry paintings. In the back were racks, wooden slats behind which oils or watercolours framed in glass could be safely transported. Rose was not quite sure what she felt about Geoff, although she had to admit she had not known him long enough to judge him fairly. Sometimes she wondered if he was making a pass, at others she thought that she was simply reading too much into the most simple statements. Time would tell, she supposed, wondering if she was in the least interested.

'Hi. Excited?' he asked, raising one eyebrow as Rose went to greet him.

'Yes.' She smiled. 'Come on in. Have you time for a coffee?'

'Regrettably, no,' he said.

Which might mean anything, Rose thought. Together they wrapped the canvases in hessian and loaded them into the back of the van. Geoff slammed the sliding door and its tinny echo reverberated in the still air. He wiped his head with a spotless handkerchief and said he would see her tomorrow. His words were accompanied with a wink, confusing Rose further.

By lunchtime the house was spotless so she set about preparing the evening meal. Fresh fish from Newlyn, naturally, had been her mother's request. Trevor, who had landed that morning, had hung a bag of fish on the kitchen door handle, knowing that Rose would be up long before the sun reached it. It contained several megrim and a crab, which must have been given to him because he and his crew fished for flat fish all year round. The crabbers only worked between Easter and September. Like many fishermen's wives, Trevor's wife, Laura, often complained there was no room in her freezer for anything else but fish.

Tomorrow she need not think of food. After the viewing, her parents were taking her out to eat. Once everything was ready she made coffee and took it out to the garden to drink. Sitting on the metal bench, she felt the sun warming her bare arms and face. Already she had a tan, which surprised most people because of the colour of her hair. She had tied it back whilst she dealt with the food but now pulled it free of its band. Her skin, nearly always devoid of make-up, was fresh, and the lines and the few stray strands of grey in her hair added character rather than aged her. She would, she realised, look very much like her mother in another twenty years' time. And in approximately another hour she would see her. She sighed with contentment and sat looking at the bay as she drank her coffee.

To her left was Newlyn harbour but only a few masts rose above the piers. Although they did not fish as a fleet most of the fishermen were taking advantage of the tides and the weather. Directly ahead was St Michael's Mount with a history stretching back to the days when the Phoenicians probably came to trade for tin. Rose loved reading about the history as well as the legends and folklore of Cornwall. She had particularly enjoyed a book about the Mount, once a stronghold of the Royalists, and how it had been defended furiously by them until they had been overcome. Because of their bravery they had been allowed to surrender as soldiers, not as prisoners. But not before his own men had had to restrain the Royalist leader, Sir John Arundel, a man then in his eighties, from blowing the whole thing up in protest. Rose smiled at the recollection as she looked over towards the Lizard Point, the southernmost tip of the country which formed one arm of the huge haven of the bay. No landmarks were visible and, in the distance, its darkly silhouetted outline looked like a sleeping monster. Around the Mount were yachts with red sails and she could hear the engine of a trawler as the sound carried across the water before it came into sight.

When the telephone rang she assumed it would be a message to say that her parents, Evelyn and Arthur Forbes, had been delayed but it was Laura Penfold, who would ring or call in for a chat at any time of day.

'Did you get the fish? I told Trevor to knock, but you know what he's like.'

Rose did. He was one of the most taciturn men she had ever met, speaking only in answer to a question or when he had something to say. 'I did. Thank him for me.'

'Have your parents arrived yet?'

'No. I'm expecting them any minute.'

'I won't keep you then. See you tomorrow night.'

Rose hung up, smiling. How like Laura to telephone about nothing. The smile widened as she heard a car turn into the drive.

It was several months since Rose's parents had visited, but they hadn't altered. Evelyn Forbes was fractionally taller than her daughter and held herself well. She was wearing a pale blue cotton shirt-waister which she had managed not to crease during the journey. Her hair, once the same shade as Rose's, had faded but it was still soft and was held back from her forehead by a narrow velvet band. She ought to have looked like a relic from the fifties, but Evelyn had a certain style which succeeded in conveying modernity.

Arthur was five inches taller than his wife and had been lean throughout the whole of his life. Deep lines etched his face which had never lost the colour acquired from working out of doors. Until he had become bored with the ever-increasing government restrictions upon farmers it was the way in which he had earned his living. He understood exactly what the fishermen were going through. Having made enough money to retire, he had done so before the time came when he would need to plough his profits into a losing venture. The farm had been sold and he and his wife had moved to a cottage in the Cotswolds where the garden had been Evelyn's idea of a dream.

Emotional tears filled Rose's eyes as first her mother then her father hugged her. 'How's my girl?' Arthur asked with a lopsided smile. To him Rose was still a girl and would always be one.

'I'm fine. And you both look so well.' Rose was lucky in that neither of her parents was infirm. They lived a life fuller than many people half their age. As an only child she had not been spoilt but she had been treated as someone special with an independent mind. It had come as a surprise to the Forbeses when she had decided to train as an artist but the decision had been hers alone and they had accepted her choice of career without question.

'We're so very proud of you,' Evelyn said. 'We've been telling absolutely everyone.'

'Your mother even went to the trouble of buying a new outfit for tomorrow night, and you know how rarely that happens these days.'

'Honestly, Arthur, you do fuss. I have plenty of perfectly nice clothes. You'd think I went around dressed like a pauper,' she added to Rose.

'Like me, you mean?' Rose glanced down at her summer uniform which consisted of jeans and a T-shirt or a denim skirt and a sleeveless blouse. That afternoon it was the latter.

Arthur looked away and her mother blushed. They had never been able to understand why such an attractive woman paid so little attention to her appearance. In the winter she wore ancient jeans or cords and faded shirts and when she worked outdoors they were topped by baggy jumpers and a waxed jacket. Some of the clothes had been David's and she felt happy in them. But when she did dress up she could look stunning.

'Come into the kitchen and we'll have some coffee. Have you had lunch?'

'Yes, we stopped at Exeter services.'

They sat at the kitchen table catching up on news while they waited for the kettle to boil. The Forbeses had been abroad since Rose had last seen them and they had brought a packet of photographs for her to look at. Evelyn got them out of her leather shoulder bag, hoping she had remembered to remove the rather saucy one Arthur had taken of her when she had stepped out of the shower unaware.

Once they had unpacked their small case Evelyn suggested they went for a walk. 'Just to be out in this weather is wonderful, but the views make me so envious of you. I know it's pretty where we are, but the sea is such a wonderful colour I could gaze at it for ages.'

'I still do. I never get used to it. Come on, let's make a start.'

Rose's parents were active and she had guessed they would want to walk after being in the car all morning. They took the cliff path to Lamorna and she hoped it would not be too far for them. Hot and tired, they did not arrive back home until after six. The terrain had been hard going, the paths narrow or steep or both. But the views had been worth it. They had rested for a while, sitting on an outcrop of rock whilst the Forbeses exclaimed anew at the clarity of the air and the spectacular blue of the sea. The gorse was in flower and added its heady scent to that of the scrubby grasses which they trampled beneath their feet. They had filled their lungs with clean air which would help to make them sleep.

They showered in turn then, refreshed, they sat in the sitting room watching the changing shades of the sea as the light altered. The windows were open but the curtains remained motionless. Bees buzzed in the lavender bush, coming and going tirelessly. The outlook was unimpeded since Rose had hacked back the hydrangea which had threatened to block it. Her brutality had done no harm, within two weeks it had started sending forth buds.

Rose opened the Scotch she had bought for her father and the gin for her mother but stuck to wine herself. Shorts always gave her a headache.

'That was delicious,' Arthur said later, wiping his mouth on one of the linen serviettes Rose had got out especially. 'You'll have to tell your mother how to do them.'

Rose had given them monkfish and bacon kebabs. She made coffee which they took through to the sitting room and was explaining how easy they were to prepare when the telephone rang. 'Excuse me,' she said, getting up to answer it. It sat on a small table not far from the window recess. Evelyn and Arthur were able to hear her end of the conversation.

'I'm glad, Jack. The more the merrier.'

Evelyn frowned. Was Rose blushing? Unlikely, she decided – she had never seen her do so before. It was probably the flush of the sun which had set and left the sky streaked with red.

'That was Jack,' Rose said unnecessarily. 'He was just confirming that he'd be able to make it tomorrow night. There was some confusion over someone's leave.'

Evelyn and Arthur were fully aware that their daughter had had an affair with him which had lasted a year. It was Rose who had broken it off because she had not been ready to commit herself in the way in which Jack had been.

At least they're still friends, Evelyn thought, watching her daughter's face for any signs to the contrary. 'You go and sit down and we'll wash up. Come on, Arthur, and in case you've forgotten, that cotton thing hanging up near the sink is a tea towel.'

Rose felt unreasonably tired, although she had to admit it had been a busy day. Perhaps a touch of nerves was responsible. It's ridiculous at my age, she thought, listening to the chink of crockery and the murmur of her parents' voices. But who cares, I've waited long enough for this. Only then did Rose realise that although she had extended Etta's invitation to include Sarah, she had not said that Joe would also be welcome. She rang Etta to tell her so, smiling when she learnt that Joe was out with Sue and wondering if there would be a wedding before the end of the year.

They were all in bed by ten-thirty; Rose in the front bedroom with the view which matched that from the sitting room window, her parents at the back where the outlook was restricted by the granite face of a cliff some yards away and the branches of a tree, now in full leaf. Seagulls screeched as darkness finally descended and the occasional chugging of a boat's engine could be heard. Rose closed her eyes knowing that she would sleep deeply and well. She smiled when she heard the low mutterings from the room across the narrow corridor whose boards would creak for a few more seconds before settling down again. It was comforting to have her parents there.

CHAPTER THREE

Trevor Penfold watched Laura pull off the yellow towelling band which held her dark curls high on her head and throw it on the dressing table. Her hair was very long and he thought she looked rather wild with it loose. In fact, he thought as she began to pull off her clothes, his wife presented quite a ferocious figure at times, hair up or down. She was an inch taller than him but he was more muscled and appeared squat. His own wavy hair was collar-length. It was a shade lighter than Laura's and grew to meet his beard. In his ear dangled a small gold cross, which he had not removed since it had been inserted when he was seventeen. 'What's the matter?' he asked, sensing her agitation.

Laura, in bra and pants, her long thin legs gleaming in the light from the bedside lamp, was chewing her lip and frowning. 'I was thinking about Rose, actually. Tomorrow, more than ever, she'll wish David was alive. I know Barry and Jack'll be there, but it's not the same, is it?'

'Isn't it?'

'Oh, honestly, Trevor, you're the most infuriating man I

know. You always answer my questions with one of your own.'

'Come here and I'll show you how infuriating I can be. Laura?'

'I'm sorry. I'm worried about her, that's all. This has been her lifetime's dream, she'd have wanted to share it with David.'

'I know.' Trevor went to the window and closed it a little then he got into bed beside his wife. Both lay rigid, deep in their own thoughts until Trevor rolled over and pulled Laura to him. 'Perhaps the exhibition will have the opposite effect, it might make her think of herself for a change. Achievement born out of hard work's a great healer at times. At least her new enthusiasm has kept her out of trouble.'

Famous last words, Laura thought as she closed her eyes, unprepared to discuss further the person she cared for more than anyone except her own family.

She and Trevor were so unalike in many ways yet their marriage mostly worked. There had been some rocky times when the only solution had seemed to be to split up, but when Trevor went to sea the rift was usually healed by the time he telephoned ship to shore, certainly by the time he landed again. He's a tough man, Laura realised, and he's seen death more than once. Men, young and old, had died fishing and there had been accidents on board which had maimed others. Laura's nature was far softer and she had struggled not to let her four sons, now all adults, take advantage of her. What would I do if I lost one of mine? she asked herself. But she could not imagine what it would feel like, all she could do was to pray that it never happened before her own death. None of them had gone to sea, at least she had that to be thankful for even if Trevor had been disappointed.

Trevor stirred then turned over and lay on his back with his hands linked behind his head.

'I thought you were asleep. You're usually flat out once you hit the pillow on landing days.'

'I was thinking about giving up fishing.'

'What?' Laura sat upright in bed, the shock registering in her face. How would they cope if he was at home all the time? They'd be at each other's throats in days. Then she saw him grin. 'Oh, Trevor, you bastard.'

But it had worked, he had made his wife laugh and now she would be more amenable to making love. Trevor reached for her. It had been a good trip and their catch had reached a good price in the market. Billy and Jan were easy to work with, they took no risks, and Joe Chynoweth, who had only been with them a short time, was turning out to be an added bonus. From hints he had dropped he might be a married man before long; that would stabilise him further, make him even more one of the team for the rest of the crew were married. Yes, all in all a good day, he thought as he stroked Laura's lean thighs.

Etta Chynoweth knew that Sarah spent too much time with her friends Amy and Roz. She did not like or trust them and she suspected they made her daughter deceitful. She blushed with shame at her hypocrisy. Was she being any less deceitful? However, on some pretext she had rung

Amy's mother that evening and was relieved to hear that Sarah was where she had said she would be, spending the night at their house.

The guests had gone to bed quite early. The combination of sunshine, sea air and long walks ensured they slept well. Many of them were unused to being out of doors all day. At eleven Etta went up. Joe had gone to meet Sue and did not know what time he would be home. It was nice of Rose to have included him in her invitation. Joe would certainly go, even if Sarah didn't.

Etta locked the front door but left the back one unbolted so Joe could let himself in with his Yale key. Tired herself, she did not hear anything until her alarm went off at six-thirty. Etta hated rushing. She liked to shower and make the bed before going down to prepare the breakfasts which she served from eight until nine.

That morning the house was unnaturally quiet. But Sarah was out and Joe, up in the attic, would be sleeping soundly if he had had a late night.

The early morning routine complete, Etta wished her guests a pleasant day as they set off to various destinations, one lot to St Ives, the other further afield to walk part of the South-West Way.

'Damn,' she swore. The doorbell had rung just as she sat down with a mug of tea.

Immediately she saw the dark shapes through the ridged glass of the front door Etta knew it meant trouble. She ought to have tried harder to discourage Sarah from seeing Amy and Roz. It was too late now. She knew she must have been right, her daughter was somehow involved with drugs. She might be excluded from school, the future she was working so hard towards ruined.

'Mrs Chynoweth?' the female WPC asked gently. Etta nodded. 'May we come in? I'm afraid there's bad news.'

Weak-kneed, she led them into the front room where her legs gave way completely. She sat on the edge of the settee with her hands resting loosely in her lap. She was numb: ashamed of her daughter, disgusted with herself for not having done anything about it.

When the male police officer coughed and told her that they were very sorry but there had been an accident, a fatal one, she took the news calmly, unable to accept that it was Joe who was dead. Even when they informed her of the probable cause of death she remained silent. The only words which ran through her head continuously were 'Not Joe, not my Joe.' How little she had known her son if this was the case. Her grief was so intense it paralysed her mind as well as her body. 'A man walking his dog found him early this morning.'

Etta seemed not to hear. 'Where's Sue?' she asked. 'Susan Veal, his girlfriend? They were together last night.' But were they? There were so many doubts now. But he had been smiling when he left her last night, smiling at the thought of seeing Sue. Etta had not even known that he had not returned, that his bed had not been slept in. What kind of a mother would they believe her to be?

'Don't worry, Mrs Chynoweth, we'll send someone to see her. There'll have to be a post-mortem.' The WPC coughed nervously before continuing. 'I think it's only fair to warn you that your son was in possession of heroin. We believe that he slipped.' She did not add that there were scuff marks and broken branches where Joe Chynoweth had desperately tried to save himself from falling.

'Where did it happen?' Etta was not sure why it mattered, but it was something to cling on to, to keep her temporarily sane.

'Between Newlyn and Mousehole, near where the quarry used to be.'

'I don't understand. Why was he there? Sue lives in Penzance. Joe said they were going out for a meal. Has anyone told her?'

They made a note of Sue's address and promised that the news would be broken to her before she heard it via the media. 'Are you sure you'll be all right on your own, Mrs Chynoweth?'

'Yes. My daughter will be home soon and I've got guests staying. I won't be alone.' But she would have liked to have been. More than anything she wanted to sit by herself and grieve. But no tears came, she was filled with a deadness which weighed her down. For the moment there was the problem of telling Sarah: despite her flippant attitude towards him, she had loved her half-brother deeply.

The police had already gone when Sarah arrived back from Amy's house. It was left to Etta to break the news.

White-faced, Sarah stared at her mother. 'You're lying, I know you're lying. Joe isn't dead. He can't be.'

'Oh, Sarah.' Etta reached out and stroked her head. It was that gesture which told Sarah it was the truth. She started to scream, her hands over her ears. Etta did not know whether this was to shut out the reality or the sound of her own hysterical voice.

Somehow they had to pass the time until their guests came back to change for the evening. Etta did not provide an evening meal. She would have to explain to four comparative strangers that her son had died and that it was impossible for them to continue their holiday with her. Naturally, she would refund all of their money and ring around to find alternative accommodation for them.

She and Sarah sat side by side, holding hands but rarely speaking. It was Sarah who made the tea that neither of them bothered to drink. After this evening there would be no one in the house except herself and her daughter. The next guests were not due to arrive for another eight days, the day following the end of what should have been her present guests' two-week holiday. It was time enough in which to cancel those bookings.

It was hot outside. The scent of the flowers in the tubs at the back wafted in through the kitchen door. They smelt sickly and made Etta nauseous. 'Sarah, I need to talk to you. There's just us now and I have to know, did you have any idea Joe was taking drugs?' Sarah shook her head and mumbled something unintelligible. 'Please talk to me. I have to know. Was he unhappy or worried about anything?'

'No. Don't ask me all these questions, I can't bear it,' Sarah sobbed. 'He was my brother and he's dead. He'd never take drugs, he hated them. What does it matter any more? What does anything matter any more?'

In a way she's right, Etta thought. Nothing would bring him back. 'It's all right, love. I didn't mean to upset you.

Shall I make us some coffee?' The idea of food sickened her but she supposed she would eventually have to eat if only to encourage Sarah to do so. As she cut bread for a sandwich she wondered if her daughter would be questioned and, if so, how she would stand up to it. Etta swayed dizzily.

'Mum?'

'It's all right, love. I'm all right.' But she wasn't. The room kept spinning wildly. The knife slipped and nicked her finger. Only when a drop of blood welled up and formed a perfect oval did her tears follow suit as they rolled down her face. Etta rested her hands on the table top and cried as though she would never stop.

'Now, what shall we do until this evening?' Rose said as she placed hot toast in front of her parents.

'What would you normally be doing?' Arthur asked, planting a kiss on her cheek.

'Working. Either painting or sketching or planning.'

'Then I'll take your mother out somewhere and we'll meet you later.'

'Good God, what for? You asked what I'd normally be doing. This is different, I want to enjoy every minute of your company. And I'm entitled to a holiday as well, you know.'

Arthur Forbes grinned widely. 'I'd hoped you'd say that. But your mother primed me. She knows how dedicated you are and insisted that we didn't interfere with your time.'

'Then she doesn't know me that well because it's all too easy to distract me.' Other people's problems especially distracted her, she realised, such as whatever it was that was troubling Sarah.

Arthur decided he would deadhead the roses whilst the women washed up.

'That's just so typical of your father. If I asked him to do that he'd have something more important to do. He's only volunteered in case he was asked to dry up.'

But he redeemed himself by offering to take them over to Carbis Bay. There they spent the day doing all the things that tourists did. They lay on towels on the powdery white sand which was hot enough to burn the soles of their feet. When Evelyn's shoulders began to turn pink they packed up and went to buy ice creams which they ate sitting on the car park wall. Then they sipped cold beer on the terrace of the hotel which sat proudly overlooking the sea before they returned to Newlyn.

'That was a lovely day,' Evelyn said as they were getting out of the car. 'I love the smell of the sun on my skin.'

Rose smiled because so did she, although there was no way in which to describe that salty, fleshy warm aroma. 'Who wants the bathroom first?' she asked, glancing at her watch. They had arrived back far later than she had anticipated.

'You do. You're the star tonight,' her mother insisted. 'Take as long as you want. We can be ready in a moment.'

'My God!' Arthur said when Rose reappeared half an hour later. 'This surely isn't my daughter? You look wonderful.'

Rose giggled. Knowing what he meant, she was not offended. The outfit she was wearing she had bought on the day Geoff Carter told her that he was willing to show her work. She had worn it only once before, on that same night when she had taken Barry Rowe out to dinner to celebrate. She had promised herself not to wear it again until the evening of the exhibition itself. It was by far the most expensive outfit in her wardrobe. Over a shimmering calf-length cream dress she wore a cream lace jacket. Her shoes were satin with ankle straps and she carried a matching handbag. She joined her parents in the kitchen where the radio was playing but being ignored.

'You look stunning,' Evelyn said, stroking Rose's hair which hung damply round her shoulders but had already started to dry.

'Who'll want to look at your paintings when they can look at you?' Arthur said wistfully.

'Honestly, Dad. You do exaggerate at times. But thank you. Shh. Listen a minute.' Something the newscaster was saying caught her attention.

'The body of a man was found this morning above the shoreline between Newlyn and Mousehole. The police have not yet issued a statement but it is believed that he fell to his death,' the voice continued.

'Oh, no. How awful,' Evelyn said. 'And it's so close to us.'

Rose nodded. 'It happens more often than you'd believe. Tourists don't understand the dangers of coastal walks.' But it seemed odd. Parts of the road were fenced and it had not been raining to make the narrow paths slippery. And it wasn't like a cliff walk, far from it. She decided not to think about it because this was her night. There would be further details in the press in the morning.

At seven they climbed into the taxi Rose had booked and made their way to the gallery in Penzance. Geoff Carter and his assistant were already there and welcomed them with glasses of wine. The door was open but there was no draught to alleviate the stuffiness of the hot summer evening.

Geoff's eyebrows arched in surprise. Rose Trevelyan had been hiding her talents in more than one direction. But he did not comment upon her appearance. 'What do you think?' he said as he took her arm and led her around.

'I can't believe it, Geoff. They look so much better now they're hung.'

'They always do. And good framing goes a long way and that's down to you.'

Unsure if he was being patronising, Rose was still aware that his expertise in knowing which paintings to place adjacent to one another made all the difference.

Her father was standing back from one of them stroking his chin thoughtfully. He beckoned to his wife. 'Well, Evelyn? What about it?'

'Yes.' She nodded. 'Yes, definitely. We'll have it.'

'You can't,' Rose gasped, horrified. 'I didn't invite you here just so you'd buy one. I'll paint you one for free, you know that.'

Geoff watched with amusement. He didn't know quite what to make of Rose, although he recognised that she could paint. 'It might be a good investment,' he suggested.

'You're bound to say that. You're on commission,' Rose retorted.

He laughed loudly whilst her parents glanced at one another in consternation.

'I'm sorry, I didn't mean to be rude. I was shocked, that's all,' Rose apologised.

'Mr Carter, we'd be very grateful if you'd put one of your red stickers on this one.'

Rose now stared at her father. He had always claimed to know absolutely nothing about art, but he obviously knew a little because that was the way it was done. A red circle would be stuck on a picture which had been sold but it would remain on the wall until after the exhibition had closed. Before she could protest further, people began to arrive. Barry Rowe was the first. He had on a grey suit which had seen better days and his tie was slightly askew. On his face was the permanently harassed expression which was no indication of how he actually felt.

'Rosie, I'm so proud of you,' he said as he kissed her cheek. 'And it's a pleasure to see you both again,' he added, addressing her parents. Geoff's young female assistant handed him a glass of wine.

She had been introduced as Cassandra. Behind Barry came Trevor and Laura, both of them smiling, determined that Rose should not miss David too badly.

Before long Rose was surrounded by her family and friends. The noise built up and she passed between small groups either in conversation or admiring her work. Her face was flushed with pleasure, she could hardly believe it was all happening. Feeling hot, she went to wash her hands in the small kitchen. When she returned to the gallery there were even more people there, including Jack Pearce who seemed to avoid catching her eye. Tall, dark and swarthy, he was, Rose realised, by far the best-looking man in the room. What she felt for him was difficult to define. He still made her skin tingle when he came near her and she enjoyed his company but she had learnt that attraction was not the same thing as love. Geoff Carter was watching their interaction with an enigmatic smirk. Rose ignored him and turned to speak to Jack. 'I'm glad you could make it,' she said.

'I told you I'd be here. I really had no idea you were this good, Rose.' He studied her face. She was happy, far too happy to have heard that the body found on the rocks was that of Joe Chynoweth. The name may not have been broadcast, but word spread rapidly in West Penwith. He would not spoil her evening by telling her: she would find out soon enough.

'Thank you,' she answered with a wry smile. 'Now let me introduce you to my parents.' She realised by the way her mother eyed him up and down that she was surprised that her daughter had turned away such a good thing. 'And this is Geoff.' He had joined them, curious to know who the man was who obviously meant something to Rose.

Jack shook his hand. Geoff Carter was an inch shorter than he was, and not in the least bohemian as some of Rose's St Ives acquaintances were. His brown hair was conventionally styled and his clothes were well cut. Even on such a warm evening he wore a lightweight jacket over his shirt and trousers. Jack was aware that men had different views from women when it came to looks but he put Geoff in the top half of the type who would appeal to the opposite sex. So this was the man Rose had talked of with such enthusiasm. He hoped it was only because he was exhibiting her paintings.

'Hi.' A new voice interrupted them.

'Hello, Maddy.' Jack grinned. This was more his idea of an artist, although, in fact, Maddy was a potter. She also produced simple wooden artefacts and fancy needlework. These goods she sold from her small shop in St Ives. Not boots tonight, he noticed, but open sandals. Her drop-waisted lavender dress almost reached her ankles and was laced down the front. Her wild hair was held in a bunch at one side of her head. The variety of Rose's friends amazed him but said an awful lot about Rose herself.

He began to enjoy himself, relaxing for once, because he was not usually much of a socialiser. Rose was chatting to Maddy. Her smile broadened as she hugged her friend but he had no idea why. It must be good news. Hopefully it would help counteract the bad. He went to speak to Trevor and Laura, with whom he had been at school. Everyone present might have listened to or watched the local news, but Jack seemed to be the only one in the room who knew the identity of the dead man, a man who was known and liked by most of them. It surprised him. But how soon would it be before Rose realised that none of the Chynoweths had turned up?

'Oh, Maddy, that's wonderful news, it's really made my day,' Rose said when Maddy had imparted her news in full. Maddy, through circumstances not of her own making, had been forced to have adopted the illegitimate child she had had as a young girl. It had warped her view of life and made her miserable. Now, after eighteen years, the thing that she had hoped and waited for had happened. The daughter she had always thought of as Annie, but who was in fact

44

called Julie, had made contact via the adoption agency and wanted to meet her natural mother.

'She asked if we can meet on neutral ground,' Maddy explained. 'I can't blame her, she's no idea what to expect. The letter only came yesterday but I knew your parents were arriving so I didn't ring right away. Anyway, you must circulate. I'll amuse Barry.'

Everyone was in conversation. Jack was with Trevor and Laura but he looked uncomfortable. Of course, she thought, they found a body. Even if the death was, as the news suggested, accidental, there would still be police involvement. Rose scanned the room, looking for Etta. She asked several people if they'd seen her, but each one answered in the negative. 'I'll ring her. Maybe she's forgotten the time,' she said to Laura.

'Don't.' Jack grabbed her arm. His expression was grim. 'Leave it for tonight, Rose.' He was aware that Trevor, Laura and Rose were staring at him, that they wanted an explanation, but he could not give them one, not yet.

Rose felt a sense of doom. Something had happened to Sarah. She had promised to speak to the girl but had left it too late. Poor Etta, her worst fears had come true.

Jack thanked Rose for inviting him and left. Other people began to follow suit.

'What was all that about?' Laura said, watching Jack's retreating back.

'I don't know for certain, but Etta's been having a few problems with Sarah.'

'She ought to get Joe to sort her out. He's no fool.'

Trevor's admiration was apparent in his voice. 'Come on, Laura, we'd better go. Rose said they've got a meal booked at nine-thirty.'

By the time she and her parents left, four paintings had a red sticker on them. 'I can't believe it. Real money at last,' Rose said as she turned to wave to Geoff who had stayed to lock up.

'You deserve it,' Evelyn commented firmly as they headed down the road towards the Promenade and the Queen's Hotel where Arthur had booked a table for dinner.

Rose forgot about Etta and Jack's serious demeanour until they were strolling home. The sky was clear, each constellation perfectly visible, and the new moon showed thinly with a slight haze outlining it. The tide was way out and so smooth not a ripple showed. Ahead were the lights of Newlyn, which looked Continental in the way the houses were grouped in tiers up the side of the bay. Why didn't he want me to talk to Etta? Rose wondered. She's my friend, she might've been glad of someone to confide in. Could Sarah have been arrested? But something more than that was bothering Jack, something he didn't want me to know. Laura and Trevor were none the wiser. No doubt they would all find out soon enough.

All three were ready for bed by the time they reached Newlyn. They had a long day ahead tomorrow: shopping and lunch in Truro, and a concert at St John's Hall in Penzance in the evening. Rose had bought the tickets in advance. It would be a treat for her parents, they always enjoyed listening to one of the many local male voice choirs.

Brushing her hair until it crackled Rose smiled at the

memory of Geoff Carter's astonished expression when she had walked into the gallery. He might not have spoken but she had read the admiration in his eyes. Life was ironic. It really was all or nothing. On several occasions since David's death she had been the object of more than one man's attention. But they never appeared singly. That evening she had been in the same room as two definite suitors and one possible admirer. Recalling the paintings which had sold, Rose shook her head. It was too good to be true. It had been a wonderful evening and a good beginning. She hoped there'd be more sales before the end of the two-week exhibition.

From her bedroom window she took her last ritualistic look at the bay and hoped that whatever trouble Sarah was in, Etta, with Rose's help, would be able to sort it out.

CHAPTER FOUR

Sarah, frightened and miserable herself, had not known how to deal with her mother's misery. She had never witnessed such overwhelming grief before, but neither had she been in a situation which warranted it. Etta had coped until their guests returned but once she had explained what had happened and they had departed, full of sympathy and understanding, she had gone to pieces. Around teatime Sarah knew that help was required. Sensibly, she decided to telephone their GP who called in after surgery had finished and prescribed some mild tranquillisers, enough to last for only a couple of days.

Etta was sleeping now, her face a little less ravaged in repose. Sarah wished she could sleep herself. Downstairs in the unusually quiet house she felt lonely and unloved. Sometime recently she had realised that although she saw Roz and Amy frequently, they were acquaintances rather than friends. When she and Roz had come across that embarrassing and sickening scene at St Ives, Roz had found it amusing; she had no idea of the pain it had caused Sarah.

Joe had been her only friend. How she wished she had been nicer to him. His affectionate teasing had been repaid with silence and it was too late now to make amends. And there was also the question of what she had seen the previous night and whether it meant anything. She could not confide in her mother, they had grown too far apart for that. But did she have the nerve to speak to Rose Trevelyan, to ask the advice of a woman she trusted? Before she could decide, the telephone rang. Sarah answered it quickly, hoping she had got there before the low but insistent burring woke her mother. It was an inquiry regarding a booking for later in the year.

Sarah explained why Etta could not come to the phone. She made a note of the name and telephone number and promised to pass on a message. 'I'm not sure when we'll be doing bed and breakfast again, but we'll let you know either way.' She was amazed at how adult and calm she had sounded, but someone had to take responsibility for their lives.

The woman who had rung to make the reservation had expressed her sympathy, asking Sarah to pass it on to Mrs Chynoweth. It was strange the way in which a contemporary of her mother had ignored her own grief. She had been treated as though the young were invulnerable, immune from pain, or perhaps it was simply that the woman could not find the right words to say to someone of her age.

Thursday night replayed itself in Sarah's head. She had not been mistaken and if Amy had heard her gasp, she had said nothing. And would she be able to bring herself to lie about the rest of that evening if the police questioned her?

They really must believe Joe's death was an accident as they had not spoken to her at all. She had imagined they would have wanted to know where she was at the very least, and possibly who his friends were. And if she was right, just what relevance did it have? I will speak to Rose, she decided, then suddenly remembered that she would not be at home because it was the opening night of her exhibition and she would be at the gallery in the company of her parents and friends. Tears filled her eyes. She and Etta and Joe should have been there too. In the morning, then. I'll go and see Rose first thing, she thought, aware of her desperate need to confide in somebody.

Switching on the television in the hope that it would distract her from memories of her brother, she sat down to watch it. It was no use. The false canned laughter made a mockery of her raw feelings. She turned it off again and sobbed, wiping her tears with her bare arm as they dampened the hair which hung over her face. He was her half-brother but it had made no difference. To Sarah he had been someone special and he had always been protective of her. How was it possible that she would never hear his laughter or his cheerful banter again? How she wished she had been nicer to him upon his return. She had no idea why she behaved badly and she was filled with self-loathing. 'There isn't a God,' she said through clenched teeth. 'There just isn't a God.' And soon there would be the funeral to face. It would be the first one she had ever attended. When Ed, the man she could just recall as her father, had died, she had been five years old and Etta had considered her too young to be present, and all her grandparents were still alive. Her maternal set were arriving on Sunday; they had been on holiday in France and, thanks to her mother's good memory, the police had been able to track them down at their hotel. They would be devastated.

Joe had been loved by her own father's parents as if he had been their natural, rather than step-grandson. They lived in Scotland and had telephoned to say they would come down and stay until the funeral. From one end of Britain to the other – it was a long journey for the elderly couple to make. No one knew where Joe's real father was, but as he had not known of the child's existence Etta saw no reason to try to find him now.

I'd have to know, Sarah thought. If it was the other way around and my mother had had me illegitimately, I'd have to try to find my real father. But Joe had shown no curiosity as to what sort of man he was or where he might be living, he had simply accepted Etta's explanation of the facts of his conception and birth and had left it at that.

It was odd that the man was French and that two of her grandparents were in France at the time of Joe's death. Sarah sat on the sofa with her eyes closed and built a fantasy around them accidentally meeting the Frenchman by whom her mother had had a child and them bringing him back to Cornwall for his son's funeral where he would fall in love with Etta and somehow make them both happy again. Better fantasy than the reality of what she might have to face.

Jack Pearce left it until Saturday morning before speaking to Trevor and Laura officially. At Rose's viewing he had refrained from mentioning what had happened because Laura was unable to disguise her feelings and Rose would have wheedled it out of her.

When he arrived at the house they were sitting at the breakfast table, plates and mugs in front of them, whilst they each read a section of the paper. But it was not the *Western Morning News* in which the dead man had now been named. 'Jack, come in,' Laura said, surprised. 'I've just made coffee. Want some?' He nodded. 'What is it?' she asked as she poured. Something had been on his mind last night. It seemed she was about to find out what.

'I expect you heard that a body was found yesterday—'

'Yes. It was on the news,' she interrupted. 'Oh, God. It's someone we know.'

Trevor looked up, several frown lines wrinkled his brow.

'I'm sorry, Laura, it was Joe Chynoweth.' He had hoped they already knew, that he would not have to break it to them.

'Joe?' Trevor's eyes, set close together, narrowed. 'They said it was an accident. If so, why are you here?'

'Because there are certain other circumstances which need investigation.'

'For Christ's sake, Jack. How long have we known each other? Cut the jargon and get on with it.'

'Joe was found in possession of drugs.'

'Not Joe. Never. Don't be a fool as well as a pompous bastard.'

'I don't like having to do this,' he said as Laura turned to hand him his coffee. He had not even given them time to let the news sink in. Their joint shock was obvious.

'Obviously I know you well enough not to imagine you were involved in the boy's death, but the way the drugs problem is escalating I need to ask you certain questions.'

'Fire away,' Trevor said, his eyes glittering with anger.

Laura, disgusted with her childhood friend, slammed his mug on the table. Its contents slopped over the rim. 'Yes, fire away, Jack. Didn't you realise Trevor's a drugs baron? That's why we live the way we do.' She waved an arm to encompass the kitchen which was in need of decoration and the mismatched china on the table.

'Laura, please. I said I hate doing this but I came myself rather than send a couple of uniforms.'

She sat down and chewed at her lip. Yes, she was angry with Jack but she was more upset than she realised at Joe's death. And he had had so much to live for.

'Did you know or even suspect what he might have been doing?'

'No. And I still don't believe it. You must've made a mistake. The police aren't infallible.' It was Laura who spoke. She paused. 'But you don't know yet if he was taking them, do you? You can't possibly know until after the post-mortem.'

'No, not for certain. Look, I have to ask, have you ever had any drugs on board?' he said, addressing Trevor.

'For Christ's sake, Jack, you know Billy doesn't even allow drink on a trip. And to save your time, the answer to almost anything you're going to ask me will be no. You should be out there finding out who supplied him, if they did, which I don't believe for one second, but if it should turn out to be the case it was no one of my acquaintance.'

Jack knew that Trevor was furious and that he was also right, but it would be like searching for the proverbial needle in a haystack. He finished his coffee and left. Much as he did not want to, he would have a quick word with Billy Cadogan and Jan Trevorrah and leave it at that. Joe's death must surely have been accidental but it was unlikely they would discover anything from the other two men. If Joe had confided in anyone it was more likely to be this man. Jack knew that most of what he was asking was superfluous, that Billy and his crew were extremely unlikely to have been involved, but he supposed he'd hoped for some sort of information, the smallest hint, maybe, as to any contacts Joe may have had. There were few secrets in West Penwith, however, but this time there seemed none to be found.

Mrs Trevorrah answered the door in a thigh-length silky dressing gown which she was hastily knotting around the middle. She was in her early twenties and had beautiful slanting eyes which altered an otherwise plain face. She looked as if she had just got out of bed because her hair was tangled and she yawned behind her hand. Jack thought lying in bed was an awful waste of a beautiful day until her husband appeared, wearing only narrow underpants. He realised what he had interrupted, which, after his interview, might not be resumed. This was an even worse waste in his opinion. But the job was the job.

'Jan Trevorrah? I'm Inspector Pearce, Devon and Cornwall police. Sorry to intrude, but I'd like to ask you a few questions.' They were standing in the hallway. No one attempted to invite him anywhere else and Jack guessed that they were anxious to get back to their Saturday morning entertainment. 'Can you tell me anything about Joe Chynoweth?'

'Such as?'

'What sort of man was he?'

'Was. Yes. Billy phoned, that's how I know. I still can't believe it.'

'Mr Trevorrah?'

'Yeah. Sorry. Good fisherman. Kept to the rules. Decent bloke to have on board or to have a drink with, but he never went too far, just a few pints now and then. But I'd never have guessed he was a user. Never in a hundred years. Mind you, I've only known him about eighteen months, since the time I started working with Billy. If you want any more than that you'll have to ask Rose.'

'Rose? What's she got to do with it?'

Jan looked startled. 'There's no need to be rude. I thought you lot went in for dealing with the public tactfully these days.'

'I apologise.' Jack was lost for words. Did Rose know these people too?

'Tell him, Rose. You went to school with him.'

Jack turned to face Trevorrah's wife. How stupid of him. There wasn't only one woman in the world with that name, especially in this particular part of the world.

'We were in the same class. He worked hard but he was never what you'd call a swot. I didn't know him that well really, but he seemed nice enough and he kept out of trouble, not like some, and everyone seemed to like him. I heard he could've gone to university if he wanted.' She shrugged and pulled her robe tightly around her body. 'We didn't really mix so I can't tell you no more than that.'

'Thank you. I won't take up any more of your time then.' Jack left with a growing feeling of disquiet. Something was wrong here. From everyone they had spoken to they had heard the same story: Joe Chynoweth was a likeable, honest young man. Hopefully, by the time he got to Camborne the results from the fingerprints taken from the small plastic packet would be waiting.

Ten-thirty; still most of the day ahead of him when he arrived at his desk, only to learn that the results he had been waiting for were negative. Partial prints had been lifted from the packet containing the heroin but they were not clear enough to be matched to Joe's or to anyone else's.

Jack read the scene-of-crime report. It added little to what had been obvious at the time. Joe had fallen through the bushes, leaving a trail of broken twigs. He had landed on the concrete at the base of the cliff, broken his neck on impact and continued to roll over the edge on to the rocks and shingle, sustaining other minor injuries on the way. Initially his death had appeared to be accidental, as, in reality, it still did. But closer investigation revealed there had been signs in the scuff marks on the dry soil that a second person, possibly even two, might have been present. Had Joe gone to meet a supplier and, drunk, or high already, slipped? If so, had whoever this man or men were, pushed him over the side? If they were involved with drugs they would not hang around to answer any questions if it had been an accident. Or was it more sinister than that? Had Joe refused to part with money and been killed?

Jack shook his head. He was beginning to accept that Joe was not a user – the post-mortem would confirm this or otherwise – but was it possible he had been a pusher? He had lived at home with his mother and sister and earned a good living fishing. He was not extravagant and could therefore have saved enough to begin buying the stuff. After that the profits would have taken care of the rest.

Does Rose know yet? he wondered. Surely she must, Laura would have rung her immediately after his visit.

Before he could ring her himself an outside call was put through to him. It was a man who called himself Douggie, although Jack knew that was not his real name. He was an informer, a man who had once served time because of being informed upon and who had now turned the tables. His information, picked up in pubs, was not always accurate but had, occasionally, proved useful. He said he wanted to meet Jack as soon as possible.

Jack rubbed the back of his neck. Would the trip be worth it? Yes, he'd have to go. Something or nothing, he thought as he left the building he'd so recently entered.

The heat in the car was unbearable. The air-cooling system blew ineffectively, wafting warm currents into his face. Jack wound down both front windows, grateful for the breeze created by the motion of the car. Ripples of heat shimmered over the sticky tarmac and made the road undulate in the distance. Sweat ran down Jack's back and dampened his shirt as he neared his destination. Once he reached Penzance he parked and walked to the cafe where he knew Douggie would be waiting. His informant was sitting with a cup of something in front of him as he scratched his grizzled head. Douggie had lived in the area all his life and knew every inch of it and many of its inhabitants but, more importantly, he also knew the movements of the ones who were of interest to the police. How no one had tumbled him was a mystery to Jack. What he did for a living was also a mystery and best not inquired into if he wasn't to lose one of the best sources of information in the area. 'How's things?'

'You know me, Inspector, plodding along the same as always.'

And one of the best sources of enigmatic replies, Jack thought, smiling because he knew the form the proceedings would take. He may as well get them over with. 'Can I get you another drink?'

'Tea, please.'

'And?'

'No, nothing to eat. Had a good breakfast. Lovely bit of hog's pudding and the whole works. An' it's too hot for any more food.' Jack was surprised. Douggie could eat all day long but he still remained unnaturally thin. Beads of sweat shone on his high, domed forehead. He had the look of a scholarly man, which he claimed he was, although there was no suggestion of this in the manner in which he lived.

Jack returned with two cups of tea and placed them on the table, watching as Douggie heaped sugar into his cup. 'You wanted to see me?'

Douggie grinned. 'You didn't come over just to pay for my tea. Well, it's like this. I overheard a bit of talk in the pub last night. Nothing definite, mind, and I only picked up bits of it, but it sounded as if there might be a boat coming in carrying more than a quota of fish.'

'I see. And the name of this boat?'

Douggie shrugged. 'No idea.'

'Trawler or yacht?'

Douggie shrugged again. 'Like I said, I didn't get all of it. They were whispering, see. Now you know fishermen, when they're talking fish or boats, what they're saying is no secret. This pair were keeping it quiet.'

'Fishermen?'

'Nope. Never seen them before. But one of them, the younger one, looked scared.'

'Any idea of time?'

'Well, I heard the word Tuesday, but that could have been referring to anything. I couldn't get hold of you last night and I certainly wasn't going to leave a message.'

'No, I was busy. Anything else you can recall?'

'Nope. Just that.'

Jack sipped his cooling tea. Why would anyone discuss such a thing within earshot? He sighed. Probably Douggie had got it all wrong. Still, he would pass on the information and leave it at that. Now and then what Douggie told him had some basis of truth and he had been helpful on several occasions when his information had led to arrests, but this sounded weird. If something big was going on, two strangers would not be stupid enough to discuss it in a local pub.

And if Douggie was right, and it was a big if, why Cornwall? The answer was obvious. There were enough coves and small bays from which a small boat could put out undetected and collect whatever was aboard a trawler before it landed. Jack slipped a note across the table. Douggie pocketed it without looking at it and without thanking him either and went back to scratching his head.

Jack left the cafe wondering if his informant had head lice.

Traffic had eased and the drive back was more pleasant. Nothing Douggie ever told him could be taken lightly but it was hard to imagine that this particular offering would amount to much. However, it was his duty to inform the relevant agencies: the drugs squad and the Joint Intelligence Cell in Plymouth. He picked up the car phone. And later I'll speak to Rose, he thought, feeling more optimistic at the idea.

Customs and Excise and the police worked in tandem to form the Joint Intelligence Cell. Although drugs were one of their concerns they were also on the lookout for smuggled tobacco and spirits. But the list of illegal goods was greater than that. There was pornography, clothes and accessories made from endangered species, rare plants and exotic birds, reptiles and animals. Ports and airports were watched and random checks made but the trade still went on. Passengers who made short trips on local airlines were closely watched. Smugglers did not stay out of the country for more than a day or so at a time. The fight went on but the officers involved knew that even if they had a tip-off and stood arm in arm along the coastline of the three counties they policed a smuggler was just as likely to come in by plane, fly right over their heads and drop the stuff in a field without even having to land. But a tip-off from a police officer of Pearce's rank certainly had to be taken seriously. They told him they would look out for any vessel unknown to them or behaving suspiciously.

Jack chatted with the operations controller for several minutes then hung up. Only later did he wonder if what he had heard had any bearing on the death of Joe Chynoweth.

CHAPTER FIVE

For months Rose had anticipated, with pleasure, the opening night of her exhibition, a highlight of her life which had been ahead of her, but she had not anticipated the anticlimax which followed on Saturday morning. One day there'll be others, she told herself. Maybe even in London. One day. I sound as if I'm young with my whole life still ahead of me, she thought. She pushed back the duvet in its white cotton cover and sat on the edge of the firm mattress.

Well, so what? There's nothing wrong in thinking that way. My mother and father take that attitude, it's the reason they've retained their youthful outlook and why they don't place limitations upon their lives. And there's nothing wrong with ambition either, it gives me a reason to get up in the mornings. She stood and stretched and went to pull back the curtains. The bay shimmered, its surface covered in dancing silver ripples which would be dazzling in an hour's time. 'It's going to be another hot one,' she said before creeping quietly along the landing to the bathroom in order not to wake her parents. Her effort was in vain. Trying to avoid the creaking board, she stepped straight on to it then the washbasin cold tap made the awful strangulated noises which emanated from it if it wasn't turned on full. It was six-thirty but Rose had always been an early riser. Broad daylight flooded the room, bouncing off the original white porcelain suite and making her squint.

Evelyn appeared in her dressing gown just as Rose was pouring her first cup of coffee of the day. 'Did I wake you?'

'No. Your father's snoring did. Didn't you hear him?'

'No.'

'I told him not to drink brandy after dinner. For some reason it always sets him off. What are the plans for today? Of course, Truro, isn't it? Do you think I'm getting senile?'

Evelyn was not forgetful, Rose knew she was making conversation rather than saying what was really on her mind. 'Out with it, Mother, what is it you're trying not to ask me?'

'How well you can read me.'

'I ought to be able to, I've known you all my life.'

Evelyn laughed and took a mug from one of the hooks beneath the hanging cupboards. 'You're not a Scorpio,' she said, puzzled, as she read the words beneath the Zodiac sign.

'No. David was.'

'Oh, Rose, I'm so sorry, that was thoughtless of me.' She put it back and took another. It would be awful if she broke it. 'That young man, Jack. Tell me to mind my own business if you like, but he seemed so right for you. I know I've only met him the once, but I just got that feeling.'

'I thought so too at one time. But we're better off at a distance.'

'And there's poor old Barry still mooning around after you.'

It was Rose's turn to laugh. 'Jack's older than Barry. You called him a young man and then say poor old Barry.'

'You know what I mean. He's always got such a hangdog expression.'

'It's just the way he is. He's okay. He'd never cope with living with someone after all these years. Especially not me. And neither would I,' she added firmly to stop what she imagined might turn out to be her mother's matchmaking attempts. 'I'm going to get dressed. The bathroom's free. Shall I take some tea up for Dad?'

'Good God! Don't you dare. He'll start expecting me to do the same.'

They were preparing to leave for Truro when the telephone rang. It was Barry Rowe, inviting them out for Sunday lunch. 'As you know, I haven't room here, Rose, but I'd like to treat you and your parents. If you haven't made other arrangements, that is,' he added quickly. He did not want Rose to accuse him of monopolising her time, a criticism he accepted as fair.

She accepted the invitation on behalf of them all and thanked him, grateful to have such a friend, one who wanted to enhance her parents' visit.

'That's extremely generous of him, Rose. Can he afford to pay for us all?'

'Indeed he can,' she replied indignantly. 'You don't know him as I do. He rarely spends anything although I try to encourage him. You've only to look at the way he dresses. He won't throw a thing out until it falls apart. And his flat!' She shook her head in disbelief. 'So don't worry about that. It'll do him good to get out his credit card. I just wish he'd spend more on himself.'

They were ready to leave. Evelyn was closing the downstairs windows when Sarah tapped hesitantly at the kitchen door. Rose took one look at her face and knew that something dreadful had happened. 'Sarah?' Gently, she led her to a chair at the kitchen table. Evelyn, who had just walked into the room, saw Rose shake her head and left again quietly.

Sarah's face was white and there were shadows under her eyes. Her whole body trembled and she seemed unable to speak.

She has come to me after all, Rose was thinking, I did not need to find an excuse to talk to her. But when Sarah spoke Rose saw how wrong she had been. This was something far worse than she had imagined.

'Joe's dead,' she said so quietly that Rose could not believe she had heard correctly.

'Joe?' Drowned, Rose thought. Another life lost to the sea. What would this do to Etta who had already buried a husband?

Sarah nodded. 'Someone found him yesterday morning. The police think he was taking drugs. Oh, Rose, it can't be true, I know he wasn't.' Tears ran down her face unheeded. Just saying it made it so much more real.

Rose gripped the back of a chair. Not Joe, she thought, just as Etta had done. Not Joe, I don't believe it. Shock and sorrow gave way to anger. Yesterday evening. Jack Pearce had attended her opening night and not said a word. He knew Etta was her friend. Had Laura and Trevor also known and not told her? Her mouth was dry but there were no words of comfort she could offer because nothing would bring back Sarah's brother. 'What on earth made them think that?' she asked instead.

'Mum said something about them finding a packet of heroin. He fell. Somewhere not far from here. He slipped down the cliff and broke his neck. Or so they said.'

'It would have been quick,' Rose said, hoping this was true. 'He wouldn't have felt anything.' She hated herself for the platitudes which Jack had once told her were all there was to offer in circumstances such as these. She understood him a fraction more in those few seconds. 'Look, I'll make us some coffee then we can talk. It helps, you know, even if it doesn't seem like it at the time. Oh, is Etta on her own?'

'Yes. She said she needed some time to herself before my grandparents arrive later today.'

'Does she know where you are?'

'Yes. Not that she cares.' More tears came into her eyes.

Rose frowned, sorry for the girl's distress and her misreading of the situation. Had Etta inadvertently allowed Sarah to think she would have preferred her younger child to have died? 'What do you mean, Sarah? She cares about you very much.'

'Not as much as her married boyfriend.' She stopped

and bit her lip but it was too late, the words had been said.

So that's it, Rose thought. I knew there was something on Etta's mind. She decided to ignore it for the moment. She spooned coffee into the filter machine and added water. 'Let's wait until the coffee's ready then we'll talk. Excuse me, Sarah, I won't be a minute.'

Rose left the room and found her parents standing side by side in front of the fireplace. They had been looking forward to the trip to Truro, now she would have to disappoint them. But Rose did not know that the shock and misery she felt was clearly visible in her face. Her parents stared at her. 'Rose? What's happened?' Arthur's eyes narrowed in concern.

'Mum, Dad, I'm really sorry but I won't be able to make Truro this morning. Etta's daughter's here. Sarah. She came to tell me that her brother's dead. Oh, heavens, I didn't mean to cry.'

'Rose, dear,' Evelyn said, taking her in her arms. 'Of course you must cry. Arthur, pour her a drink.'

'No. No, really, I'm all right,' she said as she wiped her eyes on her bare forearm. 'Sarah wants to talk to me. It all sounds a bit odd. Maybe she knows something. Would you mind if I didn't come with you?'

'Of course not,' Arthur said firmly, trying not to show how sad he felt for her. It seemed such a shame that this news had to follow the previous happy and successful night. 'Come on, love, we'll take ourselves off and leave them to chat.'

Evelyn picked up her handbag which had been lying on a chair and followed her husband out of the room. They said hello to Sarah on their way through the kitchen but left it at that, feeling it was better to say nothing to the girl as they knew neither her nor her family. Any words other than a simple greeting would have been meaningless coming from strangers.

'We'll be back around three,' Arthur said. 'I'll buy your mother some lunch.' He kissed the top of his daughter's head.

They heard the car start and reverse down the drive. 'Are they your parents?' Sarah asked, her face still tear-stained.

'Yes.'

'At least you know they love you.'

'Now, let's have that coffee, shall we?' Rose said, trying to sound businesslike. There were undercurrents in the Chynoweth family she had no idea existed. She wondered if there were any biscuits. She did not eat sweet things but occasionally bought them for guests, and they were supposed to be comforting. But by the anxious way Sarah was picking at the hem of the baggy T-shirt she wore outside her jeans, it was doubtful she would be able to face food.

'Sugar?'

'No, thanks. Just black, please.'

Rose placed the two mugs on the table and cursed silently when the telephone rang again. This time it was Jack Pearce calling to give her the news she had so very recently received. 'I know, Jack. I've just heard. Sarah's here. She came to tell me. Can we talk later?' Rose wanted to hear his side of the story, but it would have to wait, Sarah's needs were more immediate.

'I don't know what to do, Rose,' Sarah said when she returned to the kitchen. 'I don't even know if I ought to say anything at all. I can't speak to Mum, and especially not now.' She paused, unsure where to begin. 'It's about Mark, my boyfriend.'

Rose was not aware she had one and did not think Etta was either. Mother and daughter had something in common because Rose did not think Etta would have told Sarah about the man she was seeing if he was married. So how had Sarah found out?

'Well, he takes me out and, well . . .' Colour came into her face then drained away just as quickly.

'You've had sex with him?'

Sarah nodded, amazed that someone of Rose's age could say such a thing so easily. 'Yes. But sometimes I feel he doesn't like me at all. I thought he might be seeing someone else as well. I – oh, Rose, I tried to follow him.'

Rose had no idea where this was leading or why it should have upset her so much. It was no more than typical teenage insecurity. 'Go on.'

'I was supposed to be staying with Amy. Mum doesn't like her much, or Roz, but she doesn't stop me seeing them. She can't, can she? Not after what she's doing.' The bitterness was obvious.

Had Joe known about Etta's affair? Rose wondered. 'Amy and Roz, they're friends of yours?'

'Sort of.'

Sort of friends, sort of boyfriends. How different things are from the days of my youth, Rose thought before recalling her relationship with Jack. Wasn't he a sort of boyfriend? 'But you didn't stay with Amy?'

'Oh, yes, I did. I stayed the night with her, but she

was meeting someone, a boy, and told her mother she was going to the cinema with me. I made myself scarce until the time the film was supposed to end then I met her and we went back to her house together.'

Rose almost smiled, recalling similar incidents during her own teenage years. Then she remembered Joe and the reason why Sarah was there.

'Where did you go?'

'I feel so stupid now. I'd decided to try to follow Mark to see if he was meeting someone else.' There was another pause, this time longer. 'I shouldn't have come. I don't think I can tell you now. I'm sure it doesn't matter.'

It matters if she's gone to all this trouble, Rose realised. It probably matters a great deal. 'You might feel better if you do. You have my word I won't mention whatever it is to anyone without your permission.'

Sarah took a deep breath and brushed her long fair hair away from her face. 'I saw him. Mark. He was with another man. We were on the last Mousehole bus, that's where Amy lives, in Mousehole. They were just standing there, gazing out to sea. I wasn't sure it was him at first, it was dark, but when he turned round I knew for certain. I'm not sure if he saw me or not.

'You see, I'd spent several hours looking for him, I know all the places he goes to in the evenings but he wasn't at any of them. Then, suddenly, there he was, and he wasn't with another girl. I was so relieved at the time. Then, yesterday, I realised he must have been very close to the place where Joe fell.' Some of the tension had left Sarah's body now that she had voiced her concern.

'You don't seriously think Mark had anything to do with it?'

'Of course not. It was just seeing him there and – well, I don't know what to say if the police question me.'

'Just tell them the truth, Sarah. Mark can't possibly hold that against you.' Or could he? By the expression on Sarah's face it seemed that he might. But maybe that wasn't it, maybe Sarah did not want the fact that she had been jealous enough to try to follow him to come out, coupled with the deceit she and Amy had employed in telling their respective mothers they were going to the cinema. 'How old is Mark?'

Sarah's head came up and she met Rose's eyes. 'Why?' Her mug was empty. Rose got up to refill it. The sun had moved to the south. A broad stream of sunlight slanted over the kitchen floor and turned Sarah's pale hair into a halo.

'I just wondered.' Rose smiled to soften her inquiry and refilled their coffee mugs.

'He's twenty-three.'

Not a schoolboy as Rose had imagined, but a man. 'Have you known him long?'

'About six years, since I started secondary school with his sister, but we only started going out a few months ago.'

'Where does he take you?' Rose had no idea why she was asking these questions, only that something seemed wrong with the relationship.

Two spots of colour appeared across Sarah's cheekbones. 'To the pub or clubs and sometimes we go for a walk. There's a hut . . .' She stopped. Telling Rose Trevelyan what went on in that hut was taking things too far.

'Nothing changes,' Rose said to reassure her, avoiding

the mention of underage drinking. 'There were fields and canal walks and woodlands in my day. Lovers' lanes, they were called then.'

As if she had waited only for that moment for the floodgates to open, Sarah talked at length about Mark and how they spent their time. It gradually occurred to Rose that Sarah had no one else in whom to confide, she no longer trusted her own mother. She listened carefully but only because she realised that, for the moment, Sarah had put Joe's death to the back of her mind. The pain would return but a respite from it would do no harm.

'You won't say anything, will you, Rose?' Sarah said when she got up to leave. 'I mean, Mum doesn't know about Mark, and she doesn't know I know about her and that man.'

'Not a word. But remember what I said, if the police do question you, just tell them the truth.'

But Sarah did not reply. She thanked Rose for the coffee and left looking a little better than when she had arrived.

Rose watched her walk down the path. Aside from her grief there was something more than having seen Mark troubling Sarah. Leave well alone, she could hear Barry Rowe saying, although that was impossible now. Dear Barry. How good of him it was to have invited them all out. She ought to be more patient with him. But Etta, Rose realised sadly, now had a double burden to bear.

She turned and went to sit on the garden bench, smoothing down the fabric of the dress she had put on for their shopping expedition to Truro. I must see Etta, she thought, I must go to her. But Sarah had said she wanted to be alone. Ought I to telephone, she wondered, or would that seem like ducking the issue? In the end she did walk down to the house. Etta was in but she was too distraught to do more than thank her for coming.

'If there's anything I can do, anything at all, just ring me,' Rose said. She had stayed no more than ten minutes and had only a fleeting glimpse of Sarah who was outside in the garden sitting on the grass with her back to the house.

There was no cooling breeze now. The heat had built up and was heavy and enervating. The walk home made Rose hot and sticky but her mind was working overtime. Joe and drugs, never, she told herself, and she would have to tell Jack so. And Sarah? Etta had been worried that her daughter had been taking drugs and that she was holding something back. There was Etta herself with the added complication of a married man. Heaven only knew how she found time in her busy life to meet him. And then there was Maddy to whom she had not given a moment's thought, Maddy whose whole life would be changed so drastically by finding her daughter again. There was so much to think about it made her head ache. Perhaps it was better to wait until Jack rang later, to find out what was really going on. And at the back of it all was her own grief which she had managed to hide from Sarah. She had liked Joe so very much.

Evelyn and Arthur returned at two thirty. Both were a little subdued and they seemed not to have bought anything. 'We'll give the concert a miss if you'd prefer,' Arthur offered upon seeing his daughter's unhappy face.

'No, it'll help me forget for a while. Music always does that to me. Oh, that'll be Jack.' Rose reached for the phone. 'I couldn't talk this morning, not with Sarah here,' she explained quickly, hoping she had not offended him because she was anxious for news.

'I understand.'

'You can't seriously think Joe was involved with drugs?'

'They were found with the body.'

'Oh, come off it, Jack. What does that prove?'

'I'm not talking about a joint or two.'

'Well, you're wrong. Believe me, I knew that boy.'

'And so shall I by the time I've finished.'

'You see evil everywhere, Jack, that's your trouble.'

'And so would you if you did my job. Look, I know Etta's your friend, Rose, but a word of warning. Don't get involved this time. There's nothing you can possibly do which wouldn't make matters worse.'

'I see. Is that some sort of a threat?'

Jack sighed deeply. He could never win with Rose. 'Of course it isn't. I'm telling you for your own good.'

Rose slammed the receiver down. 'I'm telling you for your own good,' she mimicked more accurately than she realised. 'He just doesn't want me to prove him wrong.' There was nothing she could do to bring Joe back but Etta would find some solace if it could be proved that Joe's death was an accident, that it was nothing as sordid as Jack Pearce had suggested.

Rose had been right. As the soaring voices of the unaccompanied choir reached the rafters of the church they soothed her. She closed her eyes, shutting out everything apart from the rich notes as they swelled and receded. As always, when they sang 'Trelawney', tears filled her eyes. But they were not just for Joe, they were for everyone: for the Cornish men who had died in battle, for David and for anyone who had suffered. Yet underlying that was a sense of her own happiness, the knowledge that she had so much and that, despite everything, her life had taken on new meaning without her having done anything to deserve it. And no matter what Jack says, I can't let this rest, she decided as the choir bowed and the audience clapped and demanded an encore.

When Sarah left Rose's house on Saturday morning her temporarily lifted spirits sank again. Depression enveloped her in the same way as the heat rising from the pavement did. She knew it was partly due to her apprehension over Joe's funeral where she was sure to break down. Her grandparents had curtailed their holiday in France and were expected to arrive sometime during the evening. They would be exhausted by the non-stop drive. Her other grandparents were due to arrive tomorrow. They were making the long journey from Scotland by train.

Etta had cancelled all bookings until the end of the season, promising to return any deposits she had received. Even so, Ed's parents had opted to stay in a guest house which had ground-floor accommodation because they were too infirm to cope with stairs.

Sarah spent the rest of Saturday at home. She lay on the grass thinking and barely acknowledging her mother who she had come to believe had never loved her.

Things were easier when Etta's parents arrived. They defused the tension between mother and daughter, although Etta still had no idea why Sarah seemed to resent her so much.

'It's for you,' Etta said later in the evening when the telephone rang. She had only decided to plug the phone jack back in once her parents had arrived. Until then she had felt unable to face any more well-meaning calls. 'It's a young man,' she added with a small smile. Maybe he was the cause of Sarah's moodiness, maybe now he had rung she would become her old self again.

'Mark?' Sarah was surprised and pleased when she heard his voice. He had never telephoned her before and he obviously hadn't seen her on the bus because he sounded the same as ever and his next words confirmed it.

'Look, I haven't been in touch because I had some business to do and I've only just heard about Joe. I really am sorry. I thought I might take you out tomorrow, cheer you up a bit.'

'I'd like that.' Neither Amy nor Roz had contacted her although the news was public knowledge now.

They arranged where to meet and hung up. 'Mum, will you mind if I go out tomorrow?' she asked, suddenly finding it in herself to forgive her mother for seeing a married man now that Mark had contacted her.

'Of course not, it'll do you good.'

'That was Mark, he's—'

'Your boyfriend, dear?' her grandmother interrupted.

'Yes.' Sarah blushed and glanced up to meet her mother's gentle smile. Perhaps she had misjudged her, maybe she could have confided in her after all. But it was too late now and at least no one had shown signs of disapproval at the mention of Mark's name. Sarah, with the resilience of youth, began to feel marginally happier.

Mark Hurte put the phone down. For the first time in his life he was terrified. Too late he saw the impossibility of what Terry had told him having any basis of truth, but he had no option other than to go along with him. He had been drawn in by his charm and allowed himself to be used. To cap it all he had been unable to keep his mouth shut and now he must pay for it and so would Sarah.

There had been no reply when he'd tried her number earlier. Terry had told him to keep on trying. Mark had done so every couple of hours.

Mark had met Terry by chance. A conversation had started in a pub whilst they waited to be served with drinks. He was older than Mark by about five years and oozed confidence but he also asked a lot of questions. He had introduced himself as Terry but Mark was no longer sure it was his real name. They came across each other several more times. Mark believed he had found a friend. But Terry wanted to hear all about Sarah and, without realising it, Mark had gradually imparted her family history.

He could not verbalise his feelings for Sarah, other than that he liked being with her. She was attractive and sexy but there were times when he did not know what to say to her – although he felt that way with all females. And he had no idea how she felt about him other than that she seemed pleased to be in his company.

Perhaps if he had more confidence their relationship would improve. Sarah was never at a loss for words. Maybe if he watched her carefully he could learn from her. But for the moment he had more worrying things on his mind.

CHAPTER SIX

As promised, Barry Rowe collected Rose and her parents promptly at ten on Sunday morning. The sun continued to beat down from a cloudless sky. Barry was wearing casual trousers and a yellow, short-sleeved shirt which accentuated the whiteness of his thin arms. In deference to the occasion Rose had put on a dress for the second day running. The straight, pale green shift heightened the colour of her eyes and her auburn hair, pinned up for coolness.

'I've booked the meal for one-thirty so we've got time to do a boat trip up the Fal if anyone's interested,' Barry said, surprising Rose by his spontaneity as he took the Falmouth road.

Evelyn and Arthur agreed immediately. It would be a new experience and it might be raining next time they visited Cornwall.

Upon their arrival they decided to take the first trip going, which was not up the Fal but the Helford River. The boat was full but they had boarded early and had seats in the stern with the benefit of the breeze as they chugged slowly

81

between verdant banks. With the aid of a microphone the skipper pointed out places of interest in a deep, strongly accented Cornish voice.

'Is it really?' Evelyn whispered to Rose when the large house high up on their left was pointed out as the one upon which Daphne du Maurier had based her novel, *Rebecca*.

Rose nodded and smiled gratefully at Barry who was responsible for providing them with such entertainment.

Lunch was eaten at the Greenbank Hotel in the lovely glass-fronted dining room which overlooked the Penryn River and the village of Flushing on the opposite bank. Numerous small craft were moored on the river, many with people aboard, making repairs or about to cast off.

The tables were beautifully laid and the food superb. Only once, as he pushed his glasses back into place, did Barry glance wistfully at the second bottle of wine. But to be fair to Rose she often took her turn to drive.

Replete, they strolled down the hill past the Prince of Wales pier and entered the narrow main street to mingle with the throngs of other trippers. Some of the shops were open and the delicious aroma of pasties wafted out from the many bakers. They walked off their meal by continuing on to Customs House Quay, along past the docks and all the way up to Pendennis Castle which sat at the tip of the peninsula which formed the town. It, and St Mawes Castle, were placed strategically on either side of the Carrick Roads to defend the town from enemies.

An hour or so later they returned to the car by way of the beach road, cutting back through a side street lined with hotels.

'It was a lovely day, Barry, we can't thank you enough,' Arthur said, shaking his hand firmly when he had delivered them back to Newlyn.

'It was my pleasure.' Looking at the three suntanned faces, he beamed. It had been a good day and he had created it for them. After kissing Rose lightly on the cheek he made his way home and smothered cream on his nose and forehead, both of which were bright red, burnt by the sea breeze.

'I do hope you haven't done any supper,' Arthur groaned as he sank into an armchair. 'I don't believe I could eat another thing.'

'He'll feel differently later,' Evelyn pointed out sharply. 'Shall we have a cup of tea for now?' In the kitchen she filled the kettle and got out cups, nearly dropping one when someone rapped on the kitchen window. She smiled when she saw who it was. 'Come in. We haven't been back long. I'll tell Rose you're here.'

Jack's eyes widened when he saw her. Rose was wearing a dress. Her bare legs were smooth and brown and strands of hair wisped around her face provocatively. She still had the ability to surprise him. 'I came to apologise,' he began.

'I've just remembered something,' Evelyn interrupted swiftly and tactfully then went to join Arthur.

'Oh?'

'They did the post-mortem this afternoon. There were no illegal substances in the body. However, before you start smirking, we still believe that drugs had something to do with Joe's death.'

'The packet you found?' Rose folded her arms.

'You know about that?' How much else does she know and will keep from me out of cussedness? he thought.

She did not answer. Sarah had mentioned it casually, Rose had not believed it to be a secret.

'Anyway, I don't want us to fall out again. Apology accepted?'

Rose leant back against the edge of the sink. With her back to the window, it was hard for Jack to read her face. 'Yes. Apology accepted. You might as well have some tea, we're just making it.'

Jack grinned. It was safer than trying to kiss her, which was what he really wanted to do. 'Put so graciously, how can I refuse?'

'Go and talk to my parents and I'll bring it in.'

Jack did not stay long. Post-mortems were not one of his favourite duties, they left him feeling drained. He felt in need of a holiday, away somewhere, preferably somewhere cool. And he would have booked one if Rose would agree to go with him. He walked down to the road, where he had parked because there was no room in the drive with the two cars, without knowing that the same thought often crossed the mind of Barry Rowe.

Rose was the last to go to bed. It had been a tiring day and her parents were worn out. She tended to forget they were in their seventies. They had been abstemious since lunch but she decided she had earned a glass of wine for no other reason than it was Sunday. And an apology from Jack was worth drinking to.

Rose jumped, frowning. It was ten past eleven, late for someone to be ringing at the weekend.

84

'Rose, Sarah isn't with you by any chance, is she?' Etta asked, sounding worried.

Rose's stomach muscles tightened. 'No. I saw her yesterday morning, but I haven't heard from her since. Etta, is something wrong?'

'I expect I'm worrying about nothing. She's been out later than this before. It's just – well, my in-laws arrived today and I thought she'd make the effort to get home early. She's very fond of them.'

'I thought they came yesterday.' Rose was stalling for time as she thought.

'That was my own parents.'

'She's upset, Etta. Maybe it was too many people to face at once. Try not to worry.'

Etta sighed. 'And it looks as though you were right, there *is* a young man on the scene. Someone called Mark. That's who she went out with this morning. No doubt she'll turn up in her own good time. I hope I didn't wake you, Rose.'

'No. I wasn't in bed. Take care, Etta.'

'You, too.'

Rose picked up her glass again and sat down. What was Sarah playing at? Was she staying out late deliberately, to pay Etta back? Flaunting her own affair in the face of her mother's? Surely not at a time like this, Rose realised. And to be fair to the girl, she had let her mother know there was a young man. Her hand shook as she thought of another explanation. Sarah had not been dramatising, she had seen Mark near where Joe died and he knew it and had decided to do something about it. What on earth would it do to Etta if anything happened to her second child? Maybe Sarah had

85

lied. Why else would she have agreed to meet Mark again?

I'll ring Jack, she decided. Chewing a fingernail Rose could not decide whether her action would be construed as interference or genuine concern. But there was no answer from his flat, not even the answering machine was in operation.

If Etta's really worried she'll ring the police herself, Rose thought. But it still nagged at the back of her mind. At twelve she tried Jack again with the same result. She could not bring herself to telephone the police station. No one would take any notice of her reporting a girl missing when that girl was not her own child and the mother herself had not done so.

Too tired to think straight, she went to bed. The fresh air and sunshine had knocked her out. Even as she closed her eyes she knew there was much more to this than a simple accident.

Her dreams were troubled. Barry was offering her drugs and Jack was insisting she took them. David appeared but turned into Joe. The married man Etta was seeing was Geoff Carter who, in real life, was single. Rose woke to feel Geoff's lips on her face. She smiled with pleasure, then grinned when she realised that the lips belonged to her mother who had placed a cup of steaming coffee on the bedside table. She would have to think about that dream later.

Jack could never understand why he and Rose rubbed each other up the wrong way but accepted it as part of life.

When he reached home on Sunday evening he was

relieved to see there were no messages on his machine. To ensure none came he unplugged both it and the telephone. Slipping off his shoes he poured a measure of whisky and sank into the settee from where he could watch the comings and goings in Morrab Road. The road led down to the Promenade where the long, glass-fronted facade of the Queen's Hotel stood at right angles to it, but there was no sea view from his ground-floor flat.

It was quiet now, almost dark. Only the occasional car passed or the odd couple of tourists returning to one or other of the large granite properties which offered bed and breakfast. Some buildings, like his own, had been converted into flats and the rest housed the offices of professional people.

Douggie had said 'within the next couple of days'. Was it tonight that a boat was landing an illegal cargo? If his story was true, that is. At least Jack was satisfied that the coastguards, Customs and Excise and any other interested agency was aware of the tip-off. There was little more he could do as far as that side of things went.

He sat straighter, as if this would enable him to think more logically. According to everyone to whom he had spoken, Joe Chynoweth was almost a candidate for beatification. Accepted, people often spoke in such terms when someone died young or unexpectedly. Why, then, was that plastic bag of heroin found near his body? Had he been killed because he had refused to take part in something unlawful which involved his boat? No, it was highly unlikely – Billy Cadogan was the skipper, not Joe. However, he wondered if there was a connection between what Douggie had hinted at and Joe's death. Perhaps he should speak to Joe's sister tomorrow. Tonight all he wanted to do was to sleep and, hopefully, shake off whatever it was he felt he was coming down with . . .

When he opened his eyes it was totally dark and the empty tumbler had rolled on to the floor. This is happening too often, he reprimanded himself as he ran a hand through his thick, dark hair. I fall asleep in the chair then wake up in the night. I really do need a proper holiday, Rose or no Rose, he thought as he got into bed.

As soon as he woke he plugged in the phone. It rang immediately. He was startled and knocked the receiver off its cradle, groaning when he noticed the time. It was already after nine. His throat was raw and his limbs ached. No wonder he had been so tired over the past couple of days – he was suffering the first symptoms of the summer flu which had hit many people. He wanted nothing more than to go back to bed. 'Hello,' he croaked into the mouthpiece.

'Jack? Is that you?' Rose did not recognise his voice.

'The very same. Only suffering.'

'Hungover?' she asked sweetly, hoping to get her own back for the times he had caught her in the act of opening a bottle of wine and made her feel guilty about it.

'No. Flu.'

'Oh. Then you won't be going into work.' She sounded disappointed.

'I have to. Why?'

Overnight Rose had come to a decision. Despite her promise to Sarah, she realised she would not be able to keep

88

her name out of it, especially as the girl had not returned home last night. It was better to be honest from the start. She had spoken to Etta a few minutes earlier and she had still received no word from Sarah. 'Sarah Chynoweth came to see me yesterday and—'

'Rose, stop it right there. The case is as good as closed. The coroner'll probably give a verdict of death by misadventure later in the week and the family can then go ahead and arrange the funeral.'

'Do you want to hear what I've got to say, or not, Jack?'

'I doubt if I've much choice. And there's no need to snap.'

'I'm sorry, but I'm worried about her. Sarah told me that she saw two men near where Joe died on that night and that she knew one of them.'

'Come off it, Rose. Sarah's – what? Seventeen. Put it down to a teenage girl's imagination. She probably hasn't encountered death at first hand before, she just needs something to hold on to, some reason to explain it.'

'I knew you'd say that. Sarah's an intelligent young woman and she has every reason to be correct. She went to meet one of these men and now she's disappeared. His name's Mark.'

'What?' He had planned to speak to the girl today. This sounded serious and Rose was already one step ahead of him. He could never fathom why everyone poured their secrets into her ears.

Rose chewed her lower lip. Jack didn't know. Did that mean Etta hadn't reported it? Accepted, the police didn't search immediately for every missing teenager, especially if they'd gone off with a young man, but as she was Joe's sister, and Joe was dead, it was a different matter. 'Etta phoned me. Sarah didn't come home last night and she isn't there this morning.'

'Well, she's probably there as we speak. You know what seventeen-year-olds can be like.' Jack did not want her to know how concerned he was. He was terrified she'd get in the way – or worse, get hurt.

'For God's sake, Jack. Her brother's just died, she wouldn't go off for the night with someone and leave her mother and two sets of grandparents worried sick. Look, forget I called. And when something bad happens I hope your conscience can stand it.'

'Rose? What do you mean . . .?' but it was too late. She had already hung up. 'What the hell's she going to do next?' he asked himself as he rubbed a hand over his bristly chin. That she would do something he was in no doubt. He cursed himself. He could at least have asked for the man's full name. But when he rang back the line was engaged. He tried Penzance and Camborne police stations but neither had received a report of a missing girl. That puzzled him even more.

Only later that morning did Etta decide to telephone the police. At first she told herself that Sarah was entitled to a life of her own, that from now on she would try to treat her as an adult and, hopefully, such consideration would be reciprocated. But gradually she had to accept what she had tried to close her eyes to, that however sullen and uncooperative Sarah may have been, she had never stayed out overnight without letting her know exactly where she was.

She was transferred to Inspector Pearce's number but could give him no information other than that she thought Sarah must be with the man who had telephoned and whose name, she believed, was Mark. This was no more than Rose had told him. Neither woman knew his surname.

'Can you give me the names of any of her other friends?' Jack asked.

'She doesn't actually have that many. There's Roz Merrydown and Amy Hurte, they're her main ones.'

'Thank you, Mrs Chynoweth. We'll start looking right away. Try not to worry. Maybe she fell out with her boyfriend and stayed with one of them.' Jack shook his head as he hung up. Was Rose right? Was there more to Joe's death than they had imagined? He had been thinking over what Rose had said. She had to be right, Sarah's disappearance was more than a coincidence.

'Your relationship with that nice Inspector Pearce seems a little tempestuous,' Evelyn Forbes commented drily. She had been standing in the doorway and could not help overhearing the last part of the conversation. 'It seems to me you're ideally suited. It needs a man like that to keep you in order.' Despite the heat she looked cool and elegant in linen trousers and a striped cotton blouse.

'What's that supposed to mean? Honestly, Mother, I'm quite capable of looking after myself.'

'That's not quite what I meant, dear. Now your father and I have decided to leave you in peace for a while. There's something we'd both like to do, but we'll be back by teatime. No, don't argue, and it'll be one less meal for you to have to think about if we're not here for lunch.' She hesitated. 'Rose, I take it you'll be going to the funeral. Will it be this week, do you think?'

'I couldn't not go. But I don't know when it'll be. There isn't a date for the inquest yet, but if Jack's right, it'll be cut and dried so I expect they'll arrange it quickly.'

When Evelyn and Arthur had departed Rose refilled her mug with coffee and took it out to the garden. Sitting on the bench she tried to plan her next piece of work but her mind kept reverting to the Chynoweths. Why was Jack so stubborn? Why wouldn't he listen to her? She knew the family, he didn't. Surely he must take some action now. But did she know the family? Etta was a friend, nowhere near as close as Laura, but still a friend, and Rose had had no idea that she was conducting an affair with a married man. Still, she thought, in Etta's place, it's hardly the sort of information I'd be broadcasting even to someone I knew well. Rose's curiosity was once more aroused. She would love to have known who the man was.

The sun rose higher, warming the bare flesh of her limbs as she went over all she knew. Joe was dead, drugs found on or near his body. The police thought they were his, she knew they were not. Joe had been murdered, he had not fallen over the cliff by accident. Sarah had seen two men on the night Joe died, near where he died. She knew one of them, a twenty-three-year-old man named Mark. Sarah was now missing. What did it all add up to? That Sarah knew too much, which meant her life might be in danger. But who had wanted Joe out of the way and why? And there was the unexplained heroin. It suggested to Rose that someone was trying to set him up or trying to divert attention away from another crime. If Sarah knew Mark, then maybe Joe did too and had tried to persuade him to keep away from his sister. And where did Etta's married man come into it? If he did.

Jack and Barry were right, she really ought to keep her nose out of things. But Sarah's fear and her refusal to speak to the police were real enough. Rose knew there had to be something she could do.

'Yes,' she said with such conviction that coffee slopped over the rim of her mug and a dark, damp patch spread over her denim skirt. Rose ignored it. Of course. There was one place where Sarah might be and Jack ought to know.

'I apologise for snapping earlier,' Rose said as soon as he answered.

He had made it into work but was feeling worse than when he had woken originally. He was alert instantly. If Rose was apologising he needed his wits about him.

'And?' he asked.

'And I've remembered something else she told me.' She felt vaguely disloyal but it could hardly matter with so much at stake. 'Firstly I know that Mark's twenty-three.' She did not add that Sarah believed Mark to be her boyfriend because Jack would simply scoff and suggest the obvious.

'Yes, Mark Hurte. We spoke to his sister, Amy, although we didn't know she was his sister until this morning.'

'Oh.' Rose kicked herself mentally. One up to Jack. Sarah had mentioned a friend called Amy, she had also said that Mark was the brother of one of her friends, but Rose had not made the connection.

'She went out with Mark on Sunday, according to her mother. Etta didn't meet him, but we have to assume this was the case as he'd telephoned her the day before. On Saturday, that is.'

'Yes, so don't you see—'

'See what? Sarah claimed that Mark and another man were on the Mousehole road on the same night that Joe died. If this was true why did she confide in you and not come straight to us? And why go out with him if she really believed he was somehow involved?'

'Quite, as you would say. But think about it, Jack. Grief does strange things to people. Sarah's feeling lonely and unloved right now, she needs someone nearer her own age to talk to. Perhaps she's in love and can forgive him anything, or maybe she wants to ask him outright what he was doing there.'

'Don't you ever let up, Rose?'

'Not when I know I'm right. Pardon?' He had muttered something which sounded remarkably close to 'smug bitch'.

'Nothing. I've got to go. Don't worry, we are looking for her.'

'Do you know where to look?'

Jack groaned inwardly. 'Everywhere we can think of. Her friends weren't much help. In fact, they hardly seemed interested.' And they had something to hide, he added silently.

'Sarah told me they sometimes used an old hut.'

'Used? What for? Do they go there to take drugs, is that what you're saying?'

Rose could not answer that. Etta had suspected her of

doing so, but as far as Rose could tell, if she did there were no outward signs of it. 'The obvious, Jack.' She was not going to spell it out for him.

'And where is this hut?'

'I don't know. Hang on, if you're looking everywhere you must already know she's not at Mark's place.'

'I'm not supposed to discuss—'

'It's never stopped you before, Jack. And you know perfectly well nothing you say goes any further, not to my parents, Etta, no one.'

Jack did know. 'He hasn't been seen since Saturday evening. Neighbours confirmed he was often with another man but we can't get a halfway decent description of him.'

'She's in danger, Jack. You've got to find her. Oh God, what's this going to do to Etta?'

'Try not to worry,' he said, echoing the words he had spoken to Sarah's mother. 'We're doing our best.'

I hope it's good enough, Rose thought once she had cleared the line.

Rose was making tea, still annoyed with Jack when she looked up, surprised to see Barry Rowe in the kitchen doorway. 'Any chance of a cup?' he asked, shoving his glasses into place.

'Yes, sit down.' Barry would not sit outside, he was not a sun lover and was already suffering from yesterday's boat trip. His nose was redder still and showing early signs of peeling.

'I've left one of the girls in charge for an hour or so. I just wanted to make sure you were all right. You know, because of Joe. I know you put on a brave front yesterday in Falmouth, but I realised that was because your parents were there. That was also the reason I hardly mentioned it.'

Rose nodded. Barry had whispered a few words of sympathy and had left it at that. He had said nothing at all when he issued his invitation, which was odd because he must have known by then. Maybe he was afraid to encourage her by talking about it.

'I saw them earlier, by the way – your parents, that is. They were strolling past the shop so I knew you'd be alone. I wouldn't have come otherwise. Are you really all right?'

'Yes. And thank you, Barry.' She leant forward, about to touch his hand then thought better of it in case he misconstrued her gesture of friendship. She had to be so careful with him.

She began telling him what she had worked out but did not meet his eyes because she knew what she would read there. But, for once, Barry surprised her completely, just as he had intended to do.

'You think they've taken her to this hut?'

'Maybe not both of them. Maybe the other man is quite innocent. Maybe Sarah made the whole thing up. One thing's certain, Mark did ring her, because Etta took the call. I'm sure he and Sarah are together and I believe Jack is too, now.'

'Yes. Jack.' He paused. 'We could drive around, have a look ourselves.'

'What? Play the detectives?' After all the times he had chastised her, nagged her, warned her about how dangerous such actions were, Barry Rowe was now suggesting them.

'It won't be the first time,' he replied rather acidly. 'And if I'm with you . . .' but he did not complete the sentence. Rose might take offence if he suggested she attracted trouble when left to her own devices. 'What time are you expecting your parents back?'

'Teatime, whatever that means. Thanks, Barry, but it's too dangerous, we'd better leave it to the police.'

He hid his grin. Rose did not know how well he knew her. Had it been her suggestion to go looking, nothing would have held her back. He must remember to resort to the tactics of double-bluff in future.

Satisfied that he had achieved his aim, discouraging Rose from further involvement, Barry left to go back to the shop.

Rose felt at a loss, her emotions mixed. She had expected to spend every minute in her parents' company but they had gone out. It left her too free to worry about her friend. Even though she could have telephoned she decided to go down to the gallery and see if any more of her work had been sold. The walk would help to clear her head. She needed to put Jack Pearce and everything else out of her mind and start planning her next canvas. Before she left she changed into clean jeans and a bright, white T-shirt.

Not one, but two more paintings had red stickers on their corners and Geoff Carter seemed as thrilled as Rose was. 'You must let me take you out to dinner to celebrate when your parents have gone back,' he said.

'Thank you. I'd like that.'

Strolling back along the Promenade she tried to control the smirk on her face. I'd really like to ring Jack up and tell him about the invitation, she thought spitefully. But her grin disappeared when she recalled Sarah's plight.

There were lots of people about and none of the seats along the front was empty. Rose leant on the railings, they were always rusted with salt no matter how many times they were painted, and gazed out across the bay. Although Penzance did not boast a proper beach there were bodies in various states of undress enjoying the sun and many others in the water. Beneath the sea wall were banks of pebbles; further down below the tideline the sand was coarse and always damp. Holidaymakers usually went to Hayle or St Ives or Marazion if they desired a proper beach. The feel of the sun on her head was soothing and although Rose had half decided to try to forget the Chynoweths for the time being she found herself crossing the road and walking up the hill towards Etta's house.

The Joint Intelligence Cell in Plymouth were delighted with the information Detective Inspector Pearce had given them and were ready to act upon it. They were now aware of a beam trawler which had, ostensibly, been going about its business until the early hours of Monday morning. As far as its owner was concerned it was due to land on Tuesday morning. So why, then, had it been anchored five miles off the coast for the last twelve hours?

They could go out and search it but what they wanted was something more than what might or might not be on board. If the vessel contained drugs they wanted the men who came to collect them. Often waterproof packages were thrown over the side and floated with corks, sometimes they were sunk in crab pots with marker buoys to show where they were. By the time they were collected whoever had dropped them had disappeared.

They knew all the tricks; the swallowing of condoms filled with crack, the mothballs in a suitcase to confuse sniffer dogs, they'd seen it all. What the smugglers didn't realise was that drugs were still traceable, that urine tests could pick up the minutest amount in the system, that the dogs weren't fooled by mothballs.

But this time it was different. It appeared that the trawler was waiting for a boat to meet it. It was the most risky way of making a deal. Maybe money was changing hands. Soon they would know.

Radar would pick up the signal and track the boat as soon as it began to move. They did not want to risk being seen too soon or whatever the vessel was carrying would be jettisoned over the side.

They continued to play the waiting game throughout the whole of Monday.

CHAPTER SEVEN

On Monday morning Evelyn had suggested to Arthur that as Rose was unaccustomed to having people around her all day long, she might be grateful for a little solitude, especially in view of Joe's death and the disappearance of his sister. The Forbeses then told their daughter that they had no intention of making a nuisance of themselves by tying her down for the whole of their stay. What they didn't say was what they had admitted to each other in the privacy of their bedroom, that a few hours to themselves would be welcome. It was not as easy as it used to be to keep up with Rose's pace.

They decided to spend an hour or so looking around the shops in Penzance for a present for Rose. There were numerous small galleries and places to buy locally made crafts. Evelyn rather liked the jewellery fashioned from Cornish gemstones and polished granite but she knew her daughter did not share her taste. Unsure what would please Rose most, Evelyn finally settled upon a white china jug decorated with flowers in vivid shades of red and purple.

It had been hand-turned by a local potter and bore his signature on the base.

'It's a little, uh, garish, don't you think?' Arthur commented as they went to the desk to pay for it.

'It's cheerful. And it'll look lovely with daffodils in it in the spring. Or tulips. Besides, you've seen the collection of pottery on the shelf in Rose's kitchen, she likes basic shapes and primary colours.' Evelyn found this odd when her paintings were so subtle.

'Fair enough,' Arthur said, producing a credit card from his wallet. He wondered why his wife had bothered to ask his opinion when she was so obviously determined to have it.

When the vase had been carefully wrapped in tissue and placed in a carrier bag Arthur declared it was time to eat. 'Do you think we've made the right choice?' Evelyn asked for the second time over crab salad.

Arthur chose to ignore the 'we' and simply nodded because his mouth was full. He had no intention of going back to the shop to change their gift.

After the meal they walked down to the harbour then back along the seafront where they found a vacant seat to enjoy the lazy heat which was now tempered by the breeze off the sea. Voices drifted up from below the sea wall. Arthur closed his eyes and sighed. Here was the same question again.

'She'll be ecstatic,' he replied with a finality which Evelyn could not fail to recognise. 'Shall I pop across the road and get us an ice cream or are you up for a cream tea?'

'A cream tea sounds like a lovely idea. We shall have to

diet when we go home. Why does food always taste better when you've been out in the fresh air all day? We never seem to stop eating whilst we're down here.'

'I've no idea. Come on, let's make a move, we don't want to be back too late in case Rose has made any plans for this evening. You know what she's like.'

Evelyn smiled. Indeed she did. Always fearing they would be bored, Rose scoured the local paper and the posters in shop windows looking for simple entertainment. And there was plenty of it, Evelyn had to admit: amateur dramatics groups whose productions were far from amateur, classical music concerts, male voice choirs, female choirs, fetes and fairs, gardens to visit and the cinema in Causewayhead. What Rose didn't understand was that they were never bored in Cornwall as long as they could walk and as long as they could simply relax with their only child.

They ate their scones with clotted cream and jam and sipped China tea. It was just after four when they reached the art gallery and they still had to walk up the hill. However, they were both glad to be free of the car and knew that the exercise was doing them good.

Vehicles shimmered in the hot afternoon sun. The air was heavy with exhaust and diesel as traffic built up in Newlyn: a French pan-technicon which was being loaded with fish from the market had blocked one side of the road. Melted ice lay in puddles, ignored by the fishermen in their rubber boots. Brightly coloured plastic fish boxes clattered as they were stacked high. On the top of each pile of glistening fish was a sodden label denoting both the name of the trawler and that of the buyer.

It was later than they had anticipated when they finally reached the house. 'She's not here,' Evelyn said, puzzled, when she opened the door to silence. But both cars were in the drive, Rose hadn't gone far, she had probably decided to go for a walk. They had been given a spare key many years before and it was permanently attached to Evelyn's key ring. The house was airless and a bluebottle buzzed against the sitting room window which Evelyn opened immediately. It flew out angrily as if she was responsible for its captivity. 'I think I'll start supper, it'll give her a break. Would you like a drink?'

'Ideal. Whisky and water, please.'

She poured a generous measure and a smaller gin and tonic for herself. In the fridge were the salad ingredients which Rose had said they would be having with the thick steaks she had bought from the local butcher. The meat came from his own herds. Simple food, easy to prepare and tasty, Evelyn thought as she eyed the creamy fat and reached into the clutter of the kitchen drawer for the garlic press.

Arthur strolled out to the garden, his glass in his hand, the *Western Morning News* under his arm. He sat on the wrought-iron seat and sighed deeply with contentment. 'That view,' he said, when Evelyn joined him a few minutes later. 'No wonder she wouldn't dream of moving.'

'I know. I love our cottage dearly, and especially the garden, but in some ways I envy her.' Ahead, the bay was a blue so rich it seemed false, as if a child had attempted to depict it with poster paints. Sailing boats moved slowly in the distance and St Michael's Mount was outlined clearly against the shoreline behind it and the blue sky above it.

The rich scent of geraniums and the honeysuckle Rose had trailed along the wall filled the air. Voices of unseen people down on the road could be heard. Tourists walking back to Mousehole, they gathered, as they overheard a man and a woman discuss where they were going to eat that night.

'She's late,' Evelyn commented. 'I wonder where she's gone.'

'Probably found something she fancied drawing and is still caught up in her work. I've never known anyone who could concentrate for such long periods as our daughter. She's always been single-minded.'

Evelyn smiled and placed a blue-veined hand on his thigh. 'I'm never quite sure how we managed to produce her between the two of us. But I'm very grateful that we did.'

The position of the sun had shifted imperceptibly. Evelyn's shadow was a fraction more elongated as she got up to pour their second drink. It was a habit they had acquired since giving up farming when every minute of the day had been occupied. Once they had settled into the cottage Arthur had declared he wanted to live a more civilised life. Evelyn had agreed that two drinks before dinner was exceptionally civilised.

'It's half past five,' Arthur said, beginning to sound concerned.

'But there're hours yet until it's dark. It's probably as you said, she's wrapped up in her painting and has forgotten the time.' It was Evelyn's turn to offer reassurance but she frowned as she spoke. Her husband's anxiety had rubbed off on her. She went inside to prepare the salad and mix her own special dressing. The steaks were marinading in red wine vinegar, herbs and garlic and the kitchen table was laid for three.

'It's ten to six now, Arthur,' Evelyn said when she had put the covered bowl of salad in the fridge. 'I think we should call somebody,' she suggested nervously.

'Who?'

'I don't know. One of her friends, maybe.'

They both stood by the telephone as Evelyn dialled Laura's number followed by Doreen Clarke's. Although they had heard much about Doreen they had not met her until Friday night. She was exactly as Rose had described her, her artist's eye had missed no detail. Hayle born and bred, she had an ex-miner husband who had turned to gardening. Doreen was a plump, bolster-breasted, bustling woman who dressed twenty years out of date and wore her iron grey hair cut to chin level with an uncompromising fringe. Although the same age as Rose, she looked at least ten years older. Evelyn remembered the dress she had worn. Maroon brocade with a sweetheart neckline. She had possessed one similar back in the fifties. But Doreen was a well-meaning, generous woman and a wonderful source of gossip.

Neither Laura nor Doreen had seen Rose that day and both women sounded alarmed by the call. Barry Rowe added to their concern by sounding worried himself. It was he who suggested they telephone Jack Pearce.

'What did he mean by that?' Evelyn asked when Arthur

told her that Barry had suggested they call Jack because Rose was always getting herself into trouble.

Arthur shook his head. 'I've no idea, but I think we should take his advice.'

Evelyn turned the page of the notebook in which Rose had written addresses and telephone numbers. There were many crossings-out and squeezed-in additions. Two numbers were listed for Jack, one with an H beside it, the second with a W. She tried his home number first. He answered surprisingly quickly.

'I'm really sorry to bother you when you're off duty, but we wondered if you had any idea where Rose might be? We're not sure where or when she went out and we're just a bit worried because she isn't home yet and we told her we'd be back around four.'

Jack, with head and limbs already aching, felt another ache. But this one wasn't physical. If Rose was in trouble he would blame himself. He had known earlier that she would not let matters rest. 'She rang me this morning, twice in fact, but I haven't heard from her since. Mrs Forbes, do you know how to work her answering machine?'

'Yes, I think so.' No lights flashed, but each appliance was different. Her hopes were raised. She had not thought of trying to see if Rose had telephoned and left a message, but she felt that to press the buttons would be an intrusion of her daughter's privacy.

'Then hang up and play any messages and get back to me.'

She did so, then pressed the redial button to be reconnected with Jack. 'There's nothing, Jack, no messages at all.'

'Christ,' he muttered, hoping Mrs Forbes had not heard him. 'Look, is it all right if I come over?' It was the last thing he felt like doing, but this was so typical of Rose, becoming involved in issues best left to people like himself. But surely she would not leave her mother in a state of limbo. What could have happened to her to make her so late? He preferred not to think about that. But he ought to know better, panic was infectious. It was hardly 3 a.m. on a winter's morning.

Evelyn hung up. She was near to tears and felt rather foolish. Rose was a grown woman and it was only six o'clock in the evening but she had been distracted, more concerned than she was saying about the manner of Joe Chynoweth's death, and if Jack Pearce felt he had to come over she was certain something was wrong.

'She'll be all right,' Arthur said, putting an arm around his wife's shoulders. 'She's tough.'

'I know.' Evelyn sniffed and decided that falling apart would not help anyone.

Jack shivered despite the warmth of the evening. He could not recall having felt so ill for many years. At least it would soon be over. One by one his colleagues had succumbed to the virus. It lasted about three days. He had no idea why he was going to Rose's house and had probably alarmed her parents unnecessarily by suggesting it. Stupidly, he had forgotten to ask whether they had noticed if Rose had taken her mobile phone with her. 'Blast her. I bet she didn't,' he muttered as he eased his aching limbs into the stuffiness of the car. For the moment his interest was that of a friend. Jack did not feel a visit from the constabulary was called for; he hoped it never would be. Rose was just being untypically selfish.

'Oh, Jack, you look awful. Come in. Really, there was no need for you to come. Would you like a drink or some tea?' Evelyn was embarrassed – she had acted like an over-fussy mother.

'Tea would be fine, thank you.' He had sat down, uninvited. So used to being in Rose's house he had not waited to be asked and hoped Evelyn Forbes had not taken offence at his familiarity. She left the room seeming not to have noticed.

'What do you make of all this?' Arthur asked. He stood with his back to the fireplace, his stance not quite so upright as usual. 'Is she usually so tardy?'

'I don't know,' Jack replied ambiguously, although he was unsure what Arthur meant by 'all this'.

'There's not the remotest chance it's anything to do with that boy's death, I suppose? Only Rose – well, you know Rose.'

'Why do you ask? Has she said anything?' Maybe she had told her parents more than she had told him. And, yes, Arthur was probably right and Rose had ignored his warning; it wasn't like Rose to be late or to cause her parents or anyone else anxiety, even unintentionally.

Arthur shrugged and slipped his hands into the pockets of his lightweight trousers. 'Something Barry Rowe said, about Rose getting herself in trouble.'

They don't know, Jack thought, hardly able to believe it. They really have no idea of the risks she has taken and all that has happened to her in the past. Which made it more likely than ever that something had happened to her now. If she had gone to such lengths to protect them from the knowledge of the danger she had encountered at various times, she would not expose them to it now without very good reason.

'Did you check to see if there was a note?' Jack asked when Evelyn returned with a tray of tea upon which, he noticed, for his benefit was a bottle of aspirin.

'It was the first thing I did. All our lives the three of us have left messages by the kettle for each other. It's the first thing we reach for when we get in.'

Jack bit back his retort. He'd almost suggested that Evelyn ought to look in the fridge to see if one wasn't taped to a bottle of Frascati. 'Her car's here, she can't have gone far, that's what puzzles me. Who have you contacted?'

'We rang everyone we could think of, leaving you until last.'

'Everyone?'

'Except Mrs Chynoweth. We didn't want to bother her under the circumstances.'

'May I?' Jack indicated the telephone. Evelyn nodded. Etta's number was in Rose's book which still lay open by the phone. Her handwriting had become familiar to him during the time in which he had known her. Barely legible, it straggled across the page, frequently missing the lines. Seeing it again gave him a strange sensation in the pit of his stomach.

'Yes,' Jack said, several times, nodding to himself. 'Yes, I see. Thank you, Mrs Chynoweth.' He did not mention Joe and his own suspicions, for the moment he was more concerned about Rose.

110

'There's no news, is there? Of Sarah?'

Damn it, he thought. And I accused Rose of being thoughtless. No wonder Etta's voice had lifted upon hearing his. She must have imagined her daughter had been found. 'No, but we're still looking. It's only twenty-four hours, there's still the chance she'll turn up on the doorstep.' He did not believe that now but Etta's day must have been one of the most, if not *the* most, horrendous of her life. Every conceivable shed and outhouse was being searched but just because Sarah had said they used one it did not mean that's where they actually were.

Jack made one more call and received confirmation of where Etta had told him Rose had been earlier in the day. He turned to the Forbeses whose slumped postures gave away the depth of their anxiety. Jack did his best to smile. 'She walked down to the gallery just after lunch. Geoff Carter told me a couple more paintings have been sold and Rose was delighted.'

Evelyn nodded. Rose's success no longer mattered, she wanted her daughter back.

'From what Etta Chynoweth told me, Rose must have gone straight to her from the gallery. That was about three. She stayed for forty-five minutes or thereabouts.' Which leaves approximately two and a half hours unaccounted for, Jack thought. An awful lot could occur in that amount of time.

Arthur cleared his throat. 'Jack, I'm worried. If that girl's gone missing, then it's possible the same thing might have happened to Rose.'

It was precisely what had been going through Jack's

mind. But just then his bleeper went off and he had another call to make. I owe Douggie one, he told himself when he learnt that another, smaller vessel seemed to be approaching the trawler which had been anchored since last night.

The various officers who made up the Joint Intelligence Cell would have watched and waited patiently. They knew the score. You could keep men and vessels under surveillance for months only to be disappointed in the end. This could be something big or nothing at all. They would continue to watch until they were certain one way or another.

Men were now deployed in Newlyn, ready to search the vessel and apprehend the crew. If necessary armed men would be brought in. When drugs were involved in large quantities, those transporting them were not averse to carrying insurance by way of firearms.

So much seemed to be going on at once. Jack glanced at his watch. It was twenty to seven. 'I'd better make a move,' he said. 'We'll start looking for Rose right away. And I'll be in touch the moment there's any news.'

Evelyn showed him out. Apart from admiring his handsome face and large, well-proportioned body, she believed he was a good, decent man and he obviously cared for Rose. It was a shame their affair had come to nothing; for the first time she wondered why it had. Perhaps Geoff Carter had replaced Jack – there was certainly interest on the part of the gallery owner. 'What do we do now?' she asked when they were alone again.

'We wait patiently. There's nothing else we can do. At least Jack knows. I trust that man, he'll do his best to find her. Come and sit down and I'll pour you another drink. We can always replenish Rose's stocks later.'

One man dead, two women missing and a suspicious vessel in the bay. Were all these events connected, and had Rose already worked out the way in which they might be? Did she even know he had taken her seriously and instigated the search for Sarah Chynoweth?

He had to find Rose. Tired and ill though he was, he would help to look for her himself if necessary. Maybe both females were being held in the same place, if they *were* being held. Sarah might have used the opportunity of a grieving household to elope, for all they knew. But Rose? No, there was no way of guessing what she was up to but elopement wasn't a possibility. Jack felt a sudden flash of anger. If it did turn out to be anything to do with a man he might even kill her himself.

Sarah was trying not to cry. Life could not get any worse. On top of everything else, Mark had betrayed her. She looked at him, trying to gauge his thoughts. He seemed as scared as she was. The other, older man had hardly spoken, other than to issue instructions. He was dangerous, she knew that instinctively, although he had not hurt or threatened her in any way. Once he had left the hut but returned after an hour. Mark had not spoken to her during that time.

They had now been shut in since the previous evening. Mark, she guessed, was as much a prisoner as she was, even though he seemed not to realise it. It was stifling and every minute dragged. Then, unexpectedly, about four o'clock, the man she had heard Mark address as Terry said he had to go out again. He handed something to Mark but Sarah could not see what it was. As he did so he whispered something. Mark nodded and they were alone.

For the next half-hour she begged and pleaded with him to let her go, but Mark remained silent. 'Think of my mother if not me. She'll be worried sick, she won't be able to take it, not now. Haven't you got any compassion?' There was still no response but the fear remained in his eyes. Once, but only once, she made a lunge for the door which had been bolted on the inside after Terry left. It was then she realised that Terry had given Mark a gun. Too terrified to move, Sarah sat on the floor and waited for whatever was to happen to her.

For the first time in ages Sarah realised how much she loved her mother, and that she had been wrong about her. Etta cared for Sarah just as much as she had Joe. Now it might be too late to tell her how she felt, that she didn't really mind about the man she was seeing if it made her happy. Etta had done so much for her and Joe that Sarah tended to forget she was entitled to a life of her own just as Roz had pointed out. At that moment Sarah hated herself more than she did Mark. She had trusted him, confided in him, and together they had discovered who it was that Etta was seeing. Sarah did not want to die, she wanted to be at home with her mother's arms around her. The very idea caused the held-back tears to fall and now she could not stop them. But it no longer mattered what Mark or anyone else thought, all she wanted was to go home.

The sun began to sink but darkness was hours away. The sky and sea gradually changed colour and a half moon appeared in a lilac sky. Mark made them sandwiches but Sarah could not eat. There had been a box of groceries on the back seat of the car when he had picked her up. This had been planned. And, when they had picked up Terry late in the afternoon, she had simply taken it for granted that he was a friend of Mark's. How naive she had been.

All the innuendoes she had picked up from Amy and Roz came back to her: Mark was using her, he was selfish, she'd be better off without him. How foolish she was not to have seen it before. But there was a glimmer of hope. She had told Rose Trevelyan, had, in fact, confided in her far more than she had intended. Rose would know what to do, who to contact, she always did. Even now the police would be looking for her. But would they find her before it was too late?

Mark had told her she would be able to go home on Tuesday morning but she did not believe him. Mark seemed not to believe it himself. What could they gain by keeping her here then releasing her, knowing she would go straight to the police?

Not wishing to startle Mark, Sarah got up slowly. She sank into the musty, battered armchair and prepared to sit it out through another night.

'Oh, God!' Rose glanced at her watch. It was a few minutes to seven. Where had the time gone? And her parents, they would be worried sick. She had been so engrossed in what she was doing she had not even thought of them.

There was no question of walking home now. She ran to the phone box across the road, cursing herself for not having her mobile with her. She hated the thing but accepted that Jack had been right, it was useful, especially when she was out alone at night. First she ordered a taxi then she dialled her own number.

'Dear God, Rose, where have you been?' were her father's first words. 'Your mother's been worried sick, and so have I.'

'I'm so sorry. I really am. Look, I'm on my way back, a taxi's on its way. I'll explain when I get there.'

Stepping from one foot to the other she waited impatiently until the taxi arrived. Within fifteen minutes she was at home, unaware that Jack had passed her in his own car heading in the opposite direction. Rose saw by her parents' faces that they were trying to disguise their anger and she felt ashamed for having made them feel that way.

'So?' Evelyn said sharply as she handed her daughter a glass of wine. Beneath the tan Rose was pale and there was gooseflesh on her arms below the hems of the short sleeves of her T-shirt.

'I really am dreadfully sorry. I just lost all track of time and now I've ruined your holiday. Will you let me explain?'

'While we're eating,' Evelyn decided. 'The meal's ready, there're only the steaks to grill.'

'Oh, Mum.' Rose got up and hugged her. 'I don't deserve you.'

'And we often wonder what we did to deserve you,'

Arthur added as they went to the kitchen. But his tone spoke more of relief than anger.

Over the meal which Evelyn had prepared, thus making Rose feel more ashamed, she told them where she had been and what she had learnt.

CHAPTER EIGHT

'Well, we're home, Melly,' Roger Hammond stated unnecessarily, as he carried their bags from the garage towards the house where they had lived for the past four years.

His wife sighed. Her name was Melanie. Mel, she could live with, just, but Melly irritated her. The abbreviation conjured up a picture of a plump, cheerful country girl. She was none of those things. Roger had only started calling her that since they had moved down to the West Country. Whatever's wrong with me? she wondered. I was so close to Roger when we were away. The minute we're back from Greece I feel everything closing in on me again. They had got on so well for the past few weeks and now, more than ever, she ought to have felt happy.

Four and a half years ago each of her objections against leaving the Midlands had been squashed by reason and the disadvantages she had pointed out had been overcome by practical manoeuvres on the part of her husband until finally Melanie had agreed to the move. When Roger had

119

suggested it she had guessed his motives for wanting it, but she had imagined he meant somewhere like Bath, not too far from London and at least with a veneer of sophistication, not, as it turned out, the ends of the earth.

'It's so far from everywhere,' she had protested after they had driven down from their home in the Midlands to view the property for which an agent had sent details. When they arrived she had been aware of Roger watching her closely and knew that he had seen through her, that this last feeble stand was no more than that because she had loved the building, its grounds and the swimming pool on sight. She had always fought him every inch of the way. It was in her nature to do so, hard as she tried to compromise.

Roger fingered his bunch of keys, automatically finding the two for the front door. 'It was a good holiday. I've always liked Greece. And I'm glad you enjoyed yourself so much.'

'Yes. I did. Thank you.' Roger deserved that much, he had tried hard to make it good for her. And, in fairness to herself, she had done her best too. But she felt a bit odd, and very tired, and hoped these signs were normal and that she had not picked up some foreign bug. She glanced around, refamiliarising herself with the place while he inserted the first of the keys in the lock. He was a silent partner in something to do with steel, his actual role unclear to Melanie, but she was aware he could afford this house and the trappings.

The garden, which she loved tending, had turned out to be a bit of a disappointment. There were none of the colourful flowers she had grown at their previous house and had imagined would grow even better here. And the grass was rather parched, although it would recover. Annual bedding plants did not survive on the cliffside where they were unprotected from the salty winds and the elements. However, there were interesting shrubs and sub-tropical plants which grew to eight feet or more. Tiny pink flowers clustered tightly to their thick, woody stems from which spiky leaves also grew. There were tall Cornish palms and huge succulent-looking plants which thrived in the sandy soil, none of which she could yet name.

At the back of the house was the pool, surrounded by paving stones and earthenware pots of geraniums. This had been one of the deciding factors when Melanie agreed to buy.

A verandah ran along the front and both sides of the property which was built of stone, but not the local granite which she found unattractive. The top half of the house was timbered and painted a dazzling white; the main bedroom opened on to a small balcony from where they could look down over St Ives and out across the bay and, weather permitting, where they sometimes ate their breakfast.

'Roger?' Melanie touched his arm. She was frowning. To her right, one of the French windows was ajar; no more than an inch or so and motionless in the heat of the afternoon, but as she had turned she caught the reflection of her movement in the glass when normally she could not have done.

'Oh, hell.' Roger pushed open the front door and

listened. There were no sounds, only the muffled silence of a house that had been left empty in the heat. Even the clock in the cool, square, tiled hall had run down.

'Shall I call the police?' Melanie's face had paled beneath the Mediterranean tan. She knew how much Roger's collections were worth. But another fleeting thought had crossed her mind.

'No, I'll take a look around first. Perhaps we just forgot to close it. Stay there, Melly.' It had been very hot the day they left, possibly they'd overlooked one lock. I'm pissing in the wind, he thought. Of course we locked up properly. We both double-checked. No one went away for a month without doing so, even if they had little of value in the house.

The stairs were dappled in rainbow colours where the sun shone through the stained-glass of the porthole window on the half-landing. Roger decided to leave the upstairs until last.

The large room to the right of the hall where the window had stood open initially seemed untouched. There was no chaos, no upturned furniture or the scattered contents of drawers on the floor. If someone had broken in they had been extremely careful. Roger held his breath. Only when his eyes had adjusted to the relative dimness of the interior did he gasp. 'Oh, bloody hell!' There were blank spaces on the walls where paintings had once hung and empty surfaces where bronzes and porcelain had stood.

It was the same in each of the other downstairs rooms. My coins, he thought as sweat broke out across his forehead and beneath his armpits. The coins were in the safe in the kitchen, hidden in a box-like structure which ostensibly held the electricity meter. But the false meter on its hardboard mount swung out and to one side to reveal a wall safe with a combination known only to Roger. The real meter was under the staircase.

'Thank God.' It had not been touched.

'Roger?' Melanie had ignored his instructions and entered the house. She saw by his face what had happened and walked swiftly to the phone on the wall by the freezer. The line was dead. So was the one in the hall. Fumbling in her handbag she pulled out her mobile and rang the police. 'No,' she replied after she had explained what had happened, 'we won't touch anything.'

They waited outside in their holiday clothes in the shade of a clump of trees. They knew it could have been worse, that things might have been destroyed wantonly and that the thieves could have left a filthy mess, defecating on the carpets or urinating over the beds. It made no difference, their home had been violated and would never feel the same again.

Two cars arrived, one bearing two uniformed officers, the other a detective constable and his sergeant. In view of what Mrs Hammond had told them, that amount of manpower had been deemed necessary.

The details of how the Hammonds had found the house and an inventory of what was missing were recorded. Roger said he had a complete list of his collections in his desk and that he would double-check nothing else had been taken.

'Are you insured, sir?' the DS inquired.

'Yes, of course. Only a fool would not be.' Roger paced the sticky sweep of the tarmacked drive. Someone was on their way to take fingerprints, after which they could return to the house. He thought the officer seemed suspicious, as if Roger had arranged for the job to be done in his absence in order that he might make a claim.

'Who knew you were away?'

'I didn't tell anyone locally.' It was Melanie who answered. Her friends were in the Midlands, she had not made any new ones, only a few acquaintances.

'Nor I. My business partners knew, of course, but they wouldn't . . .' He did not complete the sentence. There was one person he had told. He cursed himself for his foolishness until he realised that what he was thinking was impossible.

'And the alarm?'

'It was deactivated, as were both telephone lines.'

It was obvious to them all that this was the work of professionals who had known exactly what to take and what to leave. They had not, like mindless vandals, left their calling card in any shape or form, and it was doubtful there would be any fingerprints other than those which could be matched to a name known to the Hammonds. At least they had not discovered the safe. But had they known it was there? Had they been disturbed? There were neighbours, albeit hidden behind high hedges. Entry had been via the front because one villa, higher up, looked down over the back. The house could not be seen from the road because the drive curved sharply.

'Who knew of your art collection, sir?' The DS was sweating profusely. The sun was at its strongest and heat seemed to have pooled within the L-shaped angle of the house and garage. He wiped his face with a dark blue handkerchief.

Roger shrugged. 'Close friends. Although I've never been foolish enough to discuss its value.'

The detective sergeant had noted more than the victims' words. Mr Hammond was probably in his fifties, his wife about ten years younger. They were attractive and wealthy, but used to money. Their clothes and the property were tasteful rather than ostentatious. Mr Hammond had a slight paunch but appeared otherwise fit and healthy and his wife was naturally good-looking without having resorted to dyeing her hair back to its original blonde in order to maintain the illusion of youth. But there were undercurrents and they seemed, in their distress, more like two strangers than a long-married couple.

'Any children?'

Roger had wondered when they would ask. It was perhaps a natural assumption that if they had teenage offspring they might have been staying at the house or one of them might have boasted about their father's possessions or mentioned to someone that their parents were away. He glanced at Melanie. She was whiter still but said nothing. 'No, Sergeant. No children.' Not any more, he added silently. 'Look, we've just returned from holiday.' He indicated their bags which still stood on the verandah. 'This could've occurred at any time during the past three weeks.'

'I don't think so. I think it was quite recently.' The sergeant had already inspected the frame of the French window. Where it had been forced the wood was splintered and sharp and still pink and raw where the paint had flaked. In the heatwave it would have darkened in colour within a day or two. 'When were you expected back?'

'Not for another week, actually. We'd booked three weeks in Greece and intended visiting old friends in Hagley on our way back. That's why we chose to fly from Birmingham.' He paused. 'But we just couldn't face it in this weather.' Roger took a few steps backwards and lowered himself on to the sawn-off trunk of a tree. It had been cut down many years previously and made an ideal seat now that the ringed surface had worn smooth. He felt weak, ready for another holiday, as if his trip to Greece had not taken place at all. What a waste. All those years of hard work, all his efforts to please Melanie. Everything he touched seemed to go wrong. Even the burglary was probably down to him.

How ironical it was. Here, where there would be less temptation for his wife, where life was slower and safer, was where they had been robbed and where he had been the one to err. Their haven had become contaminated and he began to wish they had not moved.

It was two o'clock in the afternoon when they had returned but another four hours elapsed before the police seemed satisfied and they were allowed to enter their own home.

Melanie began to unpack. She wondered if they would ever be able to pick up the pieces and why she had not told him her news when they were away. Now hardly seemed the ideal time. But perhaps it was better to wait, there were other matters to sort out first.

She sat on the end of their king-sized bed, suddenly

exhausted. It was time she made more of an effort. They had both, in different ways, sublimated their grief and, later, their bitter disappointment. She had turned to other men, Roger had begun collecting works of art. Both were substitutes for what they really wanted. It was not Roger's fault their baby had died and she had been unable to conceive again even though the experts had claimed there was nothing wrong with either of them. He had been patient, more than patient, and she had continued to punish him. And then, when her body began to signal that her menopause was imminent, she had finally accepted that she would never bear a child. This knowledge, this certainty, had mellowed her and she started to forgive him for something which had never warranted her forgiveness.

'But it might be too late,' she whispered as she stared at the lighter patch of wallpaper where a Marc Chagall had hung. She had broken their marriage vows often. The sex had meant nothing. The men had meant even less. It was escapism, nothing more. But if Roger was seeing another woman it was more than sex. She suddenly knew that she did not want to lose him. She now had the means to keep him but she did not have the heart to use them. If Roger stayed it must be because he wanted to.

The car radio crackled into life. 'We think we've located the place where the Chynoweth girl might be, sir. We've found a hut and there's a car parked to the side of it, although the officers who reported it can't get a registration mark. They're staying put, out of sight, until the rest of the team gets there. We're going to look pretty daft if the pair of them are just having a romp in the hay, so to speak.'

'Quite. But we can't take that chance. I'll join them there. Can you give me directions?' Jack had left the Forbeses only minutes earlier. Even though he was off duty he had intended going to Camborne to see what he could do to help in the search for Sarah and to instigate a search for Rose. He had wanted to be there because no one would take seriously his report of a middle-aged woman who had only been missing hours. He accelerated, anxious to arrive at the scene at the same time as the rest of the team. He prayed that no one had been hurt, and that no one would be.

Leaving Penzance he negotiated the roundabouts, cursing at the amount of traffic hot weather engendered, the dawdling tourists and the drivers who needed a half-mile gap before slotting out between cars. He indicated and took the Helston road. It was not a long journey, no more than a few miles – his destination wasn't even as far as Porthleven. He had taken Rose there in the days when they had been seeing each other regularly. It had been at the end of the season, when there were fewer tourists and it was a pleasure to wander around the fishing village without tripping over someone every few yards. They had smiled when they overheard people say how much they would love to live there. They did not see the other side, the unemployment in the county, the lack of facilities in the winter when West Cornwall seemed to close, nor did they witness the gales which swept walls of water over the high-sided harbour, where a freak wave could wash you out to sea. He could remember her smile of pleasure when, after a drink in one of the pubs, he had told her he had booked a table at a fish restaurant. After they had eaten they had walked back to the car hand in hand. I must not think of Rose, he told himself. I must remain detached.

To the right grassy slopes ran down to the edge of low cliffs beyond which was nothing but the sea. The turning was no more than a track; he had noticed it before but he had not realised there was a hut lower down. One officer, at least, was deserving of praise to have found it and, hopefully, the people they were looking for. This was supposedly private land, or so the weather-beaten sign at the entrance declared, but he had heard over the radio that no one had yet discovered who it belonged to or what it was used for. Much of the coastline around there was owned by the National Trust; this area, however, was not.

Jack took the turning and drove slowly across the bumpy tufts of grass whose roots had managed to survive in the sun-baked earth. The remaining flowers on the gorse bushes were dark yellow, almost orange, as the last of them died. Later they would bloom again. Below, shimmering in the heat of the evening, lay the bay. Surface ripples danced like a million silver fish. Sunlight glinted off the police vehicles which had been parked high up and to the left of the wooden building where they could not be seen. To the right of it the bonnet and radiator grille of a car was visible, but its number plate was plastered with mud. The hut was in surprisingly good repair considering what the elements must have thrown at it. Half a dozen men stood around, but well back and out of view. Another sat sideways in the front of a squad car, his feet resting on the grass as he listened to a message over the radio. He stood up and waved a hand. Another officer raised his in response to the signal then turned to face the shed.

The breeze was coming off the land but Jack was still able to hear what was said through a loud-hailer, some of the words louder than others as the wind briefly changed direction. 'Police. We'd like to talk to you. Please come out and identify yourselves.' There was no response. No one had approached the door and knocked. Jack assumed that this was because they did not know if whoever was inside was armed. If there was any connection between Sarah's disappearance, Joe's death and drugs they might well have a gun.

Jack parked and went to join the group of men. They might be wasting their time. The hut might be empty, the car abandoned. Even so he had a feeling that this was not the case. Please let Rose and Sarah be safe, he prayed.

'What's happening?' Jack asked in a whisper.

'We saw a movement. There's definitely someone in there.'

The man with the loud-hailer tried again. For the second time his request met with no response. It was a stand-off. They might have to take the place by force eventually, something they tried to avoid unless there was no alternative.

They waited. After what seemed like an eternity, the window opened a fraction and someone inside the hut spoke.

'Keep away if you don't want anyone to get hurt.' The voice travelled thinly towards them as the wind snatched at it greedily.

The figure moved swiftly back from the window, visible only because there must have been another source of light on the other side of the structure. The silhouette had been backlit. If you don't want anyone to be hurt, he had said. It had been the voice of a male. But the word 'anyone' gave no indication as to how many people were inside, or it could have meant one of themselves.

Jack looked at his watch. It was almost seven-fifteen. The sun was lower in the sky now, sinking down behind the mound of the coastline to his right and painting the sky in pastel shades. But it would be some time before it set completely when the purple clouds of night would rise from the horizon and the red streaks of a dying day would inflame them. It was better to have daylight on their side. Rose loved sunsets. And sunrises, and everything to do with nature. The thought of her, frightened and in danger, was enough of a spur for him to make a decision. The wrong decision. He had assumed, without checking, that Rose was inside and that it would fall upon him to rescue her. Aching and dizzy with flu, in his fear for Rose's safety he had forgotten his own position. 'All right, that's enough, let's get on with it,' he said.

'But, sir, we don't know—'

Jack snatched the loud-hailer and held it to his lips. 'You've got five minutes then we're coming in.'

The team stared at him as if he was mad. The inspector was a professional and he wasn't even on duty. They were dealing with a hostage here. He knew, as they all did, that you negotiated, no matter how long it took, and only when there was finally no other course of action or someone's life was in danger did you go in. Amongst them were men experienced in this sort of situation, trained to deal with it, the ones who should be making any such decisions. And when you did take the place, you did it with stealth, with the element of surprise and with as little risk to all parties as was possible.

Jack's shirt stuck to his back. He felt their eyes on him and knew what he had done. If things went wrong he would never be able to forgive himself. I shouldn't be here at all, he realised. He wasn't even part of the team. A combination of events had made him irrational, had made him overreact. He knew the rules and he had broken them. And you did not lie to hostage-takers. He had said what he had said and now they would have to stick to it. He felt a firm hand on his arm.

'Jack, go home.' Andy Peters, a trained negotiator, was speaking to him. He saw by Jack's grey and sweating face that he was ill.

He shook his head. 'I can't. Not now. I'm sorry.' His apology was general. He was sorry for more than what he had done.

Andy sighed. 'Okay, but keep out of things. You've done enough damage already.'

They waited until the five minutes were up then the men fanned out around the building. They had no idea how many people were inside or whether their quarry was armed. The only certainty was that there was one man who had issued a threat, but to whom it had been directed they did not know.

Jack stood back and watched. There would be

questions to answer when all this was over, possibly even disciplinary action would be taken, but that was in the future. Sick with shame he watched his fellow officers whose lives he may have endangered. What he had done must never happen again. His feelings for Rose had overcome his training and his professionalism. At that moment he both loved and hated her, hated her because his love for her had prompted him to make a stupid mistake.

And what of Douggie? What had he to do with any of this? Douggie must have been mistaken, he had misconstrued whatever he might have overheard. The man in the shed had threatened violence, he might even be armed. Something this big, something which possibly involved firearms would not have been discussed casually over a few pints. But Douggie had been right to tell him.

'Christ!'

Jack thought he heard the exclamation before the flash of light and the report of a single gunshot registered. His legs buckled and he fell to the ground but he could not understand why. He felt no pain, only a numbness in his left thigh. The sky swooped above him but all he could think of was that Rose was supposed to be the one at risk, not himself. He did not know if she was in there, or if the gunman would now kill his hostages. If she died there wouldn't be an awful lot left to live for. He finally admitted what he had always known, that he loved her.

There was shouting as blurred shapes moved past him. Through the sun-baked earth beneath his body he felt the vibration of running footsteps. Blood pounded in his ears and a face swayed in and out of focus above him. The world started to spin, kaleidoscope-fashion. There was a noise in his head like hundreds of gongs.

'Rose?' he muttered, before he lost consciousness.

CHAPTER NINE

'It's all right, love, forget it. We were worried, that's all.' Arthur touched his daughter's cheek. Since her return she had not been able to stop apologising and he could not bear to see her so crestfallen, especially as Evelyn still had what he called her pinched-lip expression; she had been angry, so had he initially but when Rose stepped out of the taxi relief had washed away his anger.

Rose smiled weakly. 'Well, I am sorry. It was thoughtless of me, not to say rude.'

'For goodness' sake, will you two stop it and eat something?' Evelyn was on her feet, filling their wine glasses. Rose had bought a special burgundy to go with the steak. 'Now, let's hear all about it,' she continued, once she had sat down. Her anger had, as always, once expressed, evaporated. 'What have you been up to this time, young lady?'

Rose turned to her with surprise. 'What do you mean by this time?'

'Ah, your good friend, Barry Rowe, hinted that you

have, over the course of the last couple of years, developed a tendency to court disaster.'

'Did he now? Well, pay no attention to that man. He fusses over me like a mother hen. He's simply overprotective. He and Jack have a lot in . . . What is it?'

'Oh, heavens.' Evelyn's hand covered her mouth and a flush spread across her prominent cheekbones. 'Arthur, we didn't let Jack know.'

'Jack?' Rose turned from one to the other. 'Let him know what?'

'That you were safe. You see, your mother and I panicked and started ringing your friends to see if anyone knew where you were,' Arthur admitted, rather shamefacedly.

'And you rang Jack?' She would never live this down and he would lecture her for weeks about consideration for others. And he would be right.

'It was Barry's idea to contact him.'

'Yes. It would be.'

'Excuse me.' Arthur stood up. 'I'd better give him a quick ring now and let him know you're safe.'

'I'll do it.' Rose patted her father's shoulder and hurried to the telephone knowing what Jack was likely to say to her parents. He would be furious and mention things she would rather not have them know. There was no answer from the flat and when she tried his number at Camborne she was told that he wasn't there either. 'Would you give Inspector Pearce a message, please? Would you let him know I'm at home,' she said without further explanation.

'Certainly, Mrs Trevelyan, if – I mean, as soon as it's

possible we'll pass on the message.' The officer's reply was hesitant.

Well, he can't have been that bothered if he's gone out for the evening, she decided after she'd hung up.

Rose paused, her hand still on the receiver, only then realising how guarded Constable Harris had sounded. What had he meant? *If* it was possible? He had corrected himself quickly enough but there was obviously something wrong. It had not struck her at the time because she had been so relieved that she had the means of letting Jack know she was safe without having to endure a tongue-lashing. She recalled vaguely a conversation when Jack had mentioned that he would like to take her and her parents out but that he wasn't sure of his movements over the next few days. Presumably he was involved in a big case which he could not discuss, even with her. Maybe that's where he was, working on it right now.

Well, she had done her duty by him, now she must explain to her parents the reason for her delay. She rejoined them and began to relate the events of the day. They had already given her their version.

'As you know, I went to see Geoff Carter. When he told me he'd sold two more of my paintings I was over the moon. It gave me a real boost and I intended coming straight home and looking over some sketches, but when I reached the end of Etta's road I knew I couldn't ignore her, not with Sarah missing on top of everything else. Although, I have to admit, I thought Sarah might have been home by then.

'I know Etta's got her family with her but I thought she might be grateful to talk to someone outside of it, someone not quite so involved, and I thought I might be able to help with shopping or something. As it happened, she was by herself. Her parents were out doing the shopping.' Rose paused to cut another cube of steak. Evelyn had cooked it exactly as she liked it, crisp and dark on the outside, pink and tender in the middle.

'And there was something else. Sarah told me that her mother was having an affair with a married man. It was news to me and I had no idea how she found out until this afternoon. On and off I kept thinking that Sarah's disappearance might have had something to do with this man.'

'How come?' Arthur asked, his fork halfway to his mouth.

'Joe's dead, the house is in turmoil and Sarah and Etta haven't been getting on lately. Sarah's got it into her head that her mother only cared about Joe – no doubt the fact that Etta doesn't approve of Sarah's friends added to her belief. And I suspect Etta had good reason to think as she did, now that I've met them.'

'Oh?' Evelyn looked up. She no longer doubted what Barry had said about her daughter. Whatever was going on with the Chynoweth family, Rose was determined to get to the bottom of it. She'd already made several discoveries of which the police seemed unaware. Rose's wine glass was empty. Evelyn refilled it, wondering how she managed to drink without ever seeming to have lifted the glass.

'I'll come to that later. Anyway, I began to think that Sarah was going through some teenage crisis. She's also got a boyfriend but Etta didn't know that until Saturday night.

Sarah's never mentioned him, let alone introduced him to her mother. Maybe she thought she would disapprove of him too. Anyway, she arranged to meet him on Sunday, with Etta's approval.

'I think Sarah, wrongly, came to the conclusion that her mother put everyone, including her married boyfriend, before her, and that's why I wanted to talk to Etta, to make sure this wasn't simply some scheme of Sarah's. I wondered if she'd stayed out on purpose either to punish Etta or to gain her attention.'

'I see,' Arthur said. 'So if her mother called in the police Sarah would know she was worried and that she cared. Sort of pitting herself against this married man for her mother's love. It would be a very cruel thing to do under the circumstances.'

'Yes. But you know what teenage girls can be like.'

'No,' Arthur said quickly. 'And I'm not sure that we ever did, not where you were concerned.'

Rose smiled and patted his hand as he reached for a slice of French bread. 'But you thought I was wonderful anyway.'

Evelyn snorted. 'Not always, my dear. Go on, you can't just stop there. You were gone ages.'

Point taken, Mother dear, Rose thought. 'Etta was in a daze. I asked her if she had been in touch with the police, which she had, and she told me they were taking it seriously. She'd already tried all her friends – yes, all right.' She had not missed the look which passed between her parents in recognition of the similar situation in which they had found themselves earlier. 'I asked her if she could think of any reason

139

why Sarah hadn't come home, but she couldn't. "I only knew of Mark's existence on Saturday," she told me.' Rose took a sip of her wine, so much talking was making her thirsty, then she continued relating the events of the rest of the afternoon.

'There are times when I think she hates me, Rose,' Etta had said sadly. 'But I honestly can't believe she'd have done something like this on purpose.'

Rose had tried to comfort her, to reassure her that Sarah did not hate her but was simply going through a patch of adolescent insecurity and really wanted nothing more than Etta's love. She had seen the longing in Sarah's eyes when they had last spoken. The girl wanted to have things put right but she was not quite mature enough to know how to go about it herself.

Etta had made them tea and they sat outside in the shade to drink it, protected by the colourful umbrella over the garden table. It was some time before Rose had the courage to ask if Sarah had said anything about seeing two men on the road on Thursday night when Joe died.

'No, not a word,' Etta had replied emphatically. 'My God, you don't think she knows something about Joe's death and that's why she's disappeared, do you?'

The more she had thought about it the more certain Rose was that this was the case. Why else would Sarah have mentioned it to her and not her mother? It was not, as she had at first imagined and Jack had later suggested, the highly charged imagination of a grieving teenager. Sarah really had seen something. 'I don't know. I'm afraid I broke my promise to Sarah, Etta. I told the police what she confided in me.' Rose ran through what Sarah had said and hoped she had imparted the facts without giving Etta further cause for alarm.

'I'm glad you did, Rose. They're likely to take more notice if they realise you are worried as well. Oh, God, I wish she was here. I need her right now and there're so many things I wish I'd said to her.' Tears filled Etta's eyes. She pulled a crumpled tissue from the pocket of her summer dress and blew her nose. 'I love her, Rose, even if she doesn't think so.'

'I know you do.'

'My parents and in-laws are doing their best, but it's hit them hard and they're not coping very well. Naturally they all expected to die before any of us. Even Ed's parents are going about in a daze. And although they're not saying anything, I know they believe that something's happened to Sarah as well.'

They had sat in silence for several minutes. Rose gave Etta time to regain her composure before asking the question which she felt, deep down, she had no right to ask, but the answer to which might matter. 'Is there anything else troubling you?'

'Not really,' she sniffed, shaking her head. But when she looked into Rose's eyes Rose knew that there was, that what Sarah had told her was true and that Etta had convinced herself that Joe's death was her punishment for having an affair with a married man. 'I . . . Oh, God. Rose, if I tell you something will you swear it'll go no further?'

'Of course it won't.'

'I've been seeing someone for just over a year. We don't meet often because it isn't possible. He's married. I've tried

141

to break it off, but I couldn't. I know it's wrong, and so does he, but there it is. I've made sure no one knows, not even Joe and Sarah. It sounds so feeble, but we got to know one another and just couldn't help ourselves. I suppose everyone in the same situation says the same thing. I was lonely and so was he. There were things in his past which had led to the marriage going wrong. He was honest enough to tell me right from the start that there was no chance of him leaving his wife.

'Once I'd got used to being on my own again I imagined I'd meet someone else somewhere along the line. It never happened, not until I met – well, not until I met this man. It isn't easy to find anyone suitable at my age. They're either already married or in a relationship or out for one thing. He's away at the moment and I'm dreading telling him about Joe. He might think he's obliged to keep seeing me out of pity.'

'I don't understand. I thought you wanted to see him.'

'Not any more. He didn't say, but I got the impression this holiday with his wife is some sort of turning point. I think he wants to try again with her, that what I've said has sunk in. I hope it works, I really don't need the extra strain at the moment. But now he might think I couldn't stand the added blow of separation.'

Rose saw how lucky she was in that respect: the men who showed an interest in her were free agents. She had no such moral decisions to make. And then she looked closely at Etta and understood her dilemma. She was large-boned and firm-featured with thick fairish hair cut in a short bob. There was nothing striking about her, nothing to make heads turn. It wasn't until you got to know her that her attraction became obvious. She was kind and gentle and a good listener and always tried to act for the best, a woman in whose company you felt important and cared for. Rose hoped that whoever the man was, he had treated her well and had wanted something more than extra-marital sex. Etta had made a moral judgement and was prepared for the affair to end. She had stopped herself from mentioning the man's name and Rose did not ask it. She listened as Etta described him and his lifestyle and saw the first spark of animation in her face since she had learnt that her son was dead. If he did break off the relationship it was going to hurt Etta more than she realised.

Forty-five minutes had elapsed when Etta's parents came back with several bags of groceries. Rose chatted to them briefly then said it was time she was going.

Her mother had not told Sarah about the affair. So how had she found out about it?

Etta walked her to the gate. 'Thanks for coming, Rose. I'll let you know if there's any news.'

'Etta, these friends of Sarah's, you're sure one of them isn't putting her up?'

'No, the police have already checked. I gave them their telephone numbers. Oh, I know Sarah thinks I disapprove of them on principle, just because they are her friends, but I don't trust them, Rose, and I'm sure they take drugs. That's why I was so worried about Sarah, I thought they'd draw her in. I just wish I'd been more tactful.'

'Amy and Roz, you mean?'

'Yes. Do you know them?'

'No, Sarah mentioned their names. Do you know where they live?'

'Yes, but Amy'll be at work now.'

Surprisingly, Etta told her where they could be found without asking Rose why she wanted to know. But Etta had more than Rose's intended actions on her mind.

'You went to see these girls?' Evelyn asked, trying not to show how aghast she was at Rose's audacity. Before they left she would find a few minutes to have a further chat with Barry Rowe. Whatever Rose thought, she did need someone to keep an eye on her or at least to try to dissuade her from some of her rasher behaviour.

Rose nodded. They had finished eating and the plates were pushed to the middle of the table. Shadows had lengthened on the lawn but there was still some daylight.

'Yes. Amy works in a pub during the afternoons. I was lucky, it wasn't busy, just a few of the regular solid drinkers. She said she didn't know that Sarah had been reported missing. I believed her. I asked her about Mark, too – he turns out to be Amy's brother, by the way, but she seems to have little to do with him.' Rose recounted the rest of the conversation.

'They've gone off together?' Amy had said, sounding surprised. 'I didn't think Mark was that serious about her.'

That statement had confirmed what Rose suspected. Mark and Sarah had not disappeared for reasons connected with romance. She had stayed only long enough to drink the half of lager and lime she had felt obliged to buy. She stepped out into the glare of sunlight and blinked. It was dazzling after the dimness of the pub. Rose began to walk, fully convinced that Amy knew nothing about any of the recent events.

Roz had been a different matter. She was temporarily unemployed, she told Rose who found her at home in her first-floor bedsit. From street level she had heard the loud rock music coming from the open upstairs window. Initially, Roz had been cagey and asked if Rose was from the police or any other agency of authority.

Rose had laughed. 'Do I look like police?' she had said, her eyebrows raised in astonishment.

'Well, you can't tell these days. The one who came before didn't look much like one either.'

Yes, Jack had said someone had already spoken to Sarah's friends. 'May I come in?'

Reluctantly Roz had said she could. Rose had sized her up immediately. She was a young woman who lived from day to day and believed in enjoying herself. For Roz the conventions did not exist and she had no fear of people's opinion of her. Dressed entirely in black, she ought to have been hot but showed no signs of being so. Her thin arms were pale beneath the T-shirt emblazoned with the name of a heavy metal band. Her dark hair was deliberately disarrayed and her purple lipstick gave her a ghoulish appearance. But it was her pupils which gave her away. They were unnaturally dilated. Etta was right, she took drugs.

'Want a beer? I've got some in the fridge.'

Rose accepted, knowing that to share something was one way of getting someone to talk.

The tabletop fridge was in an alcove which served as the

kitchen. It was half partitioned off from the main living area with a louvered pine screen which reached from floor to ceiling and which, when folded back, revealed a two-burner cooker, a sink and a washing machine.

Rose accepted the drink and repeated the conversation she had had with Amy.

'Amy's right. Mark wouldn't go off with her. He wasn't that interested.'

A second confirmation. What does he do, Amy's brother? If he had a job he would have been missed by now.

'I was right, you are from the police.' She had avoided answering the question.

'No, I'm not. Believe it or not, I'm an artist.'

Roz, perched on the side of an armchair, slid sideways into its seat and crossed her thin legs. For several seconds she appeared to be thinking. 'Yeah. I remember now. Sarah told me. I thought I knew the name. Okay, Mrs Artist, tell me why you're asking all these questions?'

Good point, Rose thought. Because she wasn't sure herself. 'Because I care about Sarah,' was the best she could come up with. 'And her mother who's worried sick.'

'Well, she would be after what happened to Joe. Joe was all right. Straight, you know what I mean? Sarah's all right, too. A bit stuffy, though. She and Mark would never have lasted. They don't have, shall we say, the same interests.'

'What makes you say that?'

'Oh, shit. Me and my mouth.'

'Is it drugs?'

'I didn't say that.' Roz looked down at her black laced

146

boots. 'If anyone ever asks I'll deny I've said it.'

'Thank you. Let's pretend that conversation never took place.' It had been an admission and both women knew it. 'Roz, if I tell you what I think happened, would you be willing to listen?'

'If you like. I haven't got anything else to do.' She examined a torn fingernail.

'I think Mark wanted Joe Chynoweth to do something illegal, something to do with his boat and drugs. Sarah saw Mark and another man in almost the very spot where Joe died that night. Maybe they had arranged to meet or maybe they followed him. I think they killed him, possibly accidentally, when he refused to do what they wanted, and I also think they may have seen Sarah on the last bus to Mousehole and that's why she's disappeared. Either she's hiding somewhere or Mark and this other man are holding her.' Rose frowned. What good would holding her do? If they intended letting her go it would only delay, not stop her going to the police. They would have to kill her to be certain they had prevented her doing so.

Roz's shriek of laughter took her by surprise. 'Mark? Involved in something that big? You've got to be joking. Look. Mrs Trevelyan, Mark's got no balls. He never has had. He can't even get a job because he goes all tongue-tied in interviews. Okay, I know I'm not exactly holding down an executive post myself at the moment, but I can always find work when I need it.

'You've got him all wrong. Mark sells the makings of the odd joint or two and a few Ecstasy tablets when he can get hold of them. Even that scares him shitless, but it's his way of trying to belong. If it wasn't for that everyone would ignore him. You can forget your theory, it just isn't on.'

Rose sipped her drink, trying not to spill it down the front of her T-shirt. She had not liked to ask for a glass, knowing that it was the in thing amongst youngsters to drink from the bottle. It was a habit she abhorred but she could hardly point this out to her hostess when the last thing she wanted to do was to antagonise her.

Rose wiped her mouth and thought for a while. 'Why was Sarah so unhappy at home?'

Roz shrugged and tilted her own bottle. She had no trouble in swallowing several inches of the liquid without choking. 'Something to do with her mother, I guess.'

'Didn't they get on?'

'You tell me. You're supposed to be the friend of the family.'

'All right. They didn't get on. What I'm asking is, why not?'

'Mrs Chynoweth is having it off with some married bloke from St Ives. It was supposed to be a secret, but there aren't any secrets down here.'

'But why did this upset Sarah so much?'

'No idea.'

'How do you know this is true?'

Roz's expression was sly. She tapped the side of her nose and grinned.

'Did Sarah tell you?'

'No. She had no need to, I saw it for myself. We were over at St Ives. There's a place where we go sometimes. It's a bit of a walk out of the town and we thought it was fairly private.'

Rose guessed what they went there to do, but made no comment.

'Anyway, there they were, Sarah's mum and this man all wrapped around each other, kissing. His hand was at the back of her head. We saw the wedding ring. I knew it was her when she turned around but we made ourselves scarce and I don't think they saw us.'

'He might be divorced but still wearing a ring.' Rose knew different but she was curious as to why Roz and Sarah had made the assumption so quickly.

'Come off it. If he was divorced she'd have taken him home, introduced him to her family and they wouldn't need to go sneaking off to isolated places for a bit of sex.'

'How did Sarah take it?'

'Oh, I don't know.' She threw back her long hair. 'I suppose not very well. She thinks a lot of her mum, whatever impression she might give, and makes her out to be some sort of saint. I think she was shocked and hurt. Anyway, they split up and Sarah said she wanted to follow him. I went along with her – once she's set her mind on something there's no stopping her. You want to see his place, Mrs T. He's got to be stinking rich. We hid in the drive and watched him let himself in. I thought people like that were car crazy and never walked. It just goes to show.' She shrugged as if she found the world a very strange place.

'We caught the bus back then. Sarah was very quiet. I haven't seen much of her since. So that's why she's probably pissed off at her mother. My mother, well, the less said about her the better. Me and my sister both buggered off as soon as we were old enough. Sarah doesn't know how lucky she is.'

'Thank you for talking to me, Roz. And thanks for the drink.' Rose stood and placed the half-empty bottle on the coffee table. She had noticed that the tiny flat was clean and tidy. Young Roz was a bit of an enigma.

Roz grinned. 'Don't thank me for something you didn't enjoy. I bet you prefer wine.'

Rose grinned back. Whatever her recreational hobbies might be she could not help liking the girl . . .

'And that was it,' Rose said. 'It was only then I realised how late it was and rang for a taxi,' she concluded, looking up to see her parents' puzzled faces. They'd had no idea of the things Rose got up to when they were not around. 'I think I'd better open some more wine, my throat's parched.'

'Or we could have coffee, dear?' Evelyn suggested.

'Of course. I'll make you both some coffee and I'll open some more wine.'

Evelyn shook her head. Rose was incorrigible. 'What do you intend to do with this information?'

Rose hesitated, the kettle in one hand, the other on the cold tap. 'I'm not sure. I mean, Jack, or someone, spoke to both girls, they'll have told him the same thing.'

'Would they?' Arthur asked.

'Why shouldn't they, Dad?'

'Well, the drugs thing for a start. They're not going to admit that to the police. And they probably wouldn't think

Etta's affair was important. They'd want to keep out of it as much as possible, especially if what you say is true and they really have no idea where Sarah and Mark have gone.

'You see, Rose, you initially suggested that Sarah's disappearance might be connected with this man Etta's been seeing, in that Sarah wished to punish her mother, but has it occurred to you that Joe's death might be connected as well?'

Rose had already filled the kettle and switched it on. Now she stood, staring at her father, the corkscrew halfway down the cork of a second bottle of burgundy. 'Oh, no. It can't be possible. Surely it can't be?'

She knew exactly what Arthur meant. Joe was straight – everyone, including Roz, had said so. If he, like Sarah, had learnt of his mother's affair he might have tried to put a stop to it, he might have threatened to tell the wife. Etta had told her that this man had no intention of leaving home for her. Such a threat, even if the affair was over, might drive a man to do almost anything. Could it be that Sarah, from her seat on the bus, had seen Etta's lover with Mark, maybe even recognised him, and that she, too, had had to be dealt with?

But where did Mark come into it? Why would this man involve someone else? Because he didn't know Sarah by sight and needed to find someone who did. This still didn't explain the packet of heroin but maybe the unknown man had used it to pay Mark to lead him to Joe and it had been dropped accidentally; maybe it had been planted on Joe to draw attention away from the real cause of his death. One thing was certain, the police needed to do a lot more investigating before the whole truth came out.

'You're right.' The cork came out of the bottle with a satisfying plop. 'I'll have to tell Jack. Let's hope he's back by now.'

Rose poured her parents' coffee and a glass of wine for herself then went to the telephone, a little worried when she discovered Jack still could not be reached.

CHAPTER TEN

When Jack opened his eyes everything overhead was still moving but swaying in a different kind of way and the sky had turned a shiny white. 'It's all right, sir, you're on your way to hospital,' a disembodied voice informed him before the face of the paramedic swam into focus. 'You were shot but you'll be all right.'

'Was anyone else hurt?' Jack struggled to sit up but a firm hand pushed him down again.

'No.'

'Thank God.' The sequence of events came back to him. It had all been his fault and he had, in all probability, ruined the whole operation.

The ambulance pulled into the bay at West Cornwall Hospital and Jack was lowered down on a stretcher and wheeled into the building. He felt impotent and impatient to learn what had happened – whether Rose and Sarah were safe, whether Mark Hurte and the second man had been arrested – but no one here was able to tell him and if the officer who had accompanied him knew, he wasn't saying.

The ambulance crew had called ahead to say that the bullet had exited the flesh and were told that it could be dealt with locally rather than at Treliske Hospital in Truro.

It seemed an eternity to Jack before his wounds were cleaned and dressed yet he had been attended to promptly. He had been lucky, he was told after he was examined, the bullet had sliced through the fleshy part of his thigh and he did not need surgery. Whoever had fired that gun had either wanted him incapacitated or else was a very bad shot if they had aimed to kill. Then Jack realised it was more likely that whoever had shot him had panicked, had possibly not even meant to fire.

'It's going to hurt once the local anaesthetic wears off,' the casualty doctor warned him. 'I'll give you enough painkillers to get you through a couple of days. After that go and see your GP.' He had shaken his head, half in despair, half in relief, when Jack insisted he was well enough to go home. The inspector ought to stay in overnight for observation; on the other hand, the free bed would be welcome. Within less than two hours of his arrival at the hospital Jack was on his way home, sitting uncomfortably in the back of a police vehicle, his thigh throbbing in rhythm with each beat of his heart.

It was several minutes before he could bring himself to ask the outcome of his mistake.

'One man under arrest, sir, and the girl's unharmed.'

One man? The girl? Were there only two people in that hut when he had believed there were four?

'Just the two of them,' the officer confirmed. 'The boy

was scared stiff. Shaking like a leaf, apparently, and ready to spill the beans.'

'Do you know what happened?'

'Yes, sir. Some of it, what I heard over the radio whilst they were seeing to you. After the lad fired that shot he went to pieces. Threw out the gun when he was asked to and came out crying, the girl by his side. She was shaken up badly, barely able to speak, so I don't know her side of the story. They took Hurte to Camborne and he's being interviewed now. Home, I take it, sir?'

As much as he would have liked to be in on the interview, Jack knew it was impossible. Weakened with flu, and in pain, he would only repeat his earlier error of judgement and ruin things for a second time. 'Yes. Home, please.'

The hospital had loaned him a stick which Jack felt foolish and clumsy using. When, assisted by the officer who had driven him, he entered his front door he found it hard to accept that it was still not late, only ten o'clock. So much had happened in the last three and a half hours. 'Thanks,' he said. 'I'll be fine now.' But he had to grit his teeth to make it into the living room.

Leaning against the table he pulled the white plastic pharmacy container containing the rest of the painkillers from his pocket. He had a choice – take one and go to bed, or forgo it and have a large whisky and hope he didn't regret it later. He had been warned of their strength and knew it was unwise to mix them with alcohol.

Beside the whisky bottle was his favourite cut-glass tumbler. Heavy-based, it tapered up into thin glass which chinked when tapped with a fingernail. It was decorated with delicate tulips which, in comparison with the glass, were slightly opaque. It had been a present, one of a pair given to him by his colleagues when he left Leeds and returned to Cornwall. Since that time the second glass had broken in much the same way as his marriage had done. Marion had remarried but had never prevented him from seeing the boys as often as he wanted when they were young. Looking back, his marriage to Marion seemed to have taken place in a different lifetime. The boys were men now and had their own lives, but they visited him just as often as they had done in their childhood. His decision to move back to Cornwall had been the reason Marion left him, no one else had been involved on either side. She hated the West Country just as Jack had hated city life and she had moved back to Leeds.

'If you can't stand it here, why did you ever leave?' she had often asked him when he complained.

'Because I needed to know.' It was true. He had not wanted to end up never having been anywhere or done anything. So he had discovered he wasn't happy outside Cornwall and returned with the wife he had met and married in Yorkshire. But just as he had been unable to settle, neither had Marion in her new home. Within two years they had separated.

Jack wondered why he was thinking of her now when he so rarely did. Then he remembered and smiled at the irony. Marion had never been able to relax when he was on duty, always imagining the worst, the knock on the door to say he had been hurt or killed in the cause of duty.

He never had been, not until now. If Marion knew, she would appreciate the black humour of the situation. One of her reasons for agreeing to their move west was that she thought he'd be safer and the children would have better lives.

'Damn.' There were messages on the answering machine. He hobbled towards it, ignoring the pain.

'DC Green here, sir. Message from a Mrs Trevelyan. It's a bit cryptic but she says she's at home now.'

'Oh, you bitch,' Jack said as his breathing quickened. 'You sodding bitch.'

He played the second message. 'Jack, it's me, Rose. I need to speak to you. Will you ring me tonight, no matter how late?' He'd been shot because of her and now she was ringing as though nothing had happened. He sank into a chair and took several deep breaths, his fury at her nonchalance hurting almost as much as his leg. It was thanks to her that he was in such pain. No, that was unfair. He had not been shot because of her, the reason had been his feelings for her and his own stupidity. Rose was not to blame. He would very much like to know exactly where she had been during the time she was supposedly missing.

But at the same time he wanted to go over to Newlyn and wring her neck.

The whisky was having its effect more rapidly than usual because of his state of mind and the temporary weakness of his body. He picked up the telephone and rang for a taxi. He would have it out with her once and for all and then he would be shot of her for ever. A one-sided relationship was no use to anyone.

It was easier said than done. For a start he had to ask the driver to go as far up the drive as the two cars parked there allowed because he would never have made it on foot, even with his stick. And then there were Rose's parents. He had hoped they might be in bed.

All three were seated around the kitchen table, their supper dishes stacked but not washed. Their faces were serious.

'Jack, come in,' Rose said when she looked up and saw his figure pass the window and pause in the open doorway. The air was heavy and oppressive and there was no cross-draught to alleviate it. 'I'm so glad you're here. We've been talking about Joe and Sarah and – Oh!' She took two steps backwards. 'What's happened, Jack? You're hurt. Come and sit down.' She reached for his arm and guided him to the remaining empty chair.

Grim-faced, wondering what on earth he was thinking of coming here at this time of night with a very large whisky under his belt, Jack did as Rose said. 'Sarah's safe,' were the first words he spoke as he lowered himself carefully into the hard-backed kitchen chair, his left leg extended straight in front of him.

'Thank goodness. What a relief for Etta.' Rose, too, sat down, brushing her loosened hair back in a familiar gesture.

Jack saw that it was a relief for Rose, too, because tears came into her eyes. Her father reached across the table and held her hand.

'We've all been worried,' Arthur said. 'So many odd things have been happening.'

'And Mark Hurte's been arrested and charged.' Rose had noticed he had been injured but she still hadn't asked why one trouser leg was pinned together, wadding and bandaging visible between the cut seam, and why he was carrying the hospital-issue walking stick.

'With what?'

'Abduction, possession of an unlicensed firearm and—'

But realisation dawned. Rose stared at his leg, her mouth wide open. 'He shot you?'

Jack nodded. 'I'll get over it.' He paused. 'I thought you were with them,' he said quietly.

There was a stunned silence as the implications sank in. Rose and her parents guessed that he had risked his life for her. He allowed them to think it: it was, in part, true. But he could not bring himself to own up to the fact that he should not have been there to start with and that he had made a dreadful mistake. It was not only his own life he had risked. Deep down he was no different from Rose, he realised.

'Rose, dear, I think you ought to let Jack know why you wanted to speak to him then he can either do something about it or go home to bed which is where, in my opinion, he should be right now. Can I get you something, Jack? A hot drink, or something stronger?'

To hell with it, he thought. It might prove to be a long and painful night but he would not be working in the morning. 'A whisky would be very welcome, if you have it.'

'I think we'll all have something.' Evelyn went off to pour their drinks, leaving behind undercurrents she had no hope of interpreting and another awkward silence. It was Jack who broke it.

'Your parents contacted me to say you had not come home. They sounded so worried I had no option but to take what they said seriously. Then, when I heard that someone believed they had found the place where the Chynoweth girl might be hidden, I imagined they'd either got you as well or you knew more than you were saying and had got there ahead of me.'

It was, in its way, a flattering statement. It meant Jack did not doubt her capabilities of deduction, whatever he might say to the contrary. But she still felt the need to make excuses. 'Yes. My mother said she'd rung you, and she did try to get back to you, or, at least, I did. I rang the station and I left a message,' she added defensively. 'But Jack, I wasn't that late. I mean, it wasn't the middle of the night or anything, I was only late by an hour or so.'

'They were worried, Rose. They acted in what they thought were your best interests.'

Here we go, she thought. Someone's taken a shot at the man, might even have killed him, but that's irrelevant, there's no way he's going to let me off a lecture. 'It was a misunderstanding. I apologise if it caused you to get things wrong.'

Colour flooded Jack's face. She could not possibly know what he had done. No, it was Rose's way of offering an apology without actually meaning it. She had managed to make him the guilty party as usual.

Evelyn returned with the drinks on a small silver tray and handed them round. 'Tell him, Rose. Tell Jack everything that you told us earlier.'

Once more she went through what she had learnt

from Amy and Roz, hesitating only when she mentioned Etta's affair. 'I had no idea, she didn't even hint at it,' Rose admitted, but loyalty to her friend stopped her from mentioning what she had learnt from Maddy Duke earlier that evening.

Jack listened without comment, realising that Rose did not know about the trawler which was under constant surveillance. But then, there were things she had told him which he had not known, and maybe more she had not told him. He had been aware of her hesitation at one point in the narration. It would be typical of Rose to hold something back. Yet all that she suspected was possible and showed that there might be more than one incident involved here. 'Who is this man?'

'Does it matter?' Rose was biting the end of her hair, a sure sign that she was prevaricating.

'Of course it does, after what you've suspected. Ah, you do know who it is.' He realised by her question that she did.

Rose blushed. Etta had enough on her plate without having to face local gossip. And if the affair was over why risk breaking up a marriage? Then she saw Joe as he had been on that Sunday lunchtime when he had talked of the sea and she knew that for his sake Jack had to know the whole truth.

Inhaling deeply she began. 'Maddy rang me. Maddy Duke. That's when I knew I had to leave a message for you, you had to know tonight. But I really hoped I could keep his name out of it, for Etta's sake.' Jack nodded, wishing she would get to the point. He ran a hand through his hair signalling impatience then moved his leg a few inches to the left. 'I don't know if I told you but Maddy's daughter has finally made contact. Anyway, she told me on the night we were all at Geoff's gallery then rang tonight to ask if I'd like to meet her.'

'Is this relevant?'

'Yes. That was the reason why Maddy rang, you see, but the conversation turned into something else. I said I wasn't sure I could make it this week because my parents are here until Thursday and, at the time, I didn't know that Sarah was safe and I wanted to be on hand if it turned out to be bad news and Etta needed me. Maddy had heard of Joe's death, of course, but she didn't realise I was a friend of the family.

'Anyway, I was explaining what happened to Maddy when she interrupted me. I could hardly believe what I was hearing, Jack.'

He sat back with folded arms as Rose related the main points of the conversation . . .

'Etta?' Maddy had said, sounding surprised when Rose explained she was Joe's mother.

'Do you know her?'

'No. But I know the name. It's unusual, that's why I remembered it.'

Rose had taken notice then. Etta's boyfriend lived in St Ives, Maddy Duke worked and lived there too, perhaps she knew him. 'Where did you hear it?'

'In the shop. A customer wanted a gift made. One of my necklaces – you know the ones I make from wood?'

Rose did. Maddy was capable of carving the most

intricate designs on tiny blocks then stringing them on thongs. It was not the sort of jewellery which appealed to Rose, she liked more feminine pieces, but they sold well, especially to younger customers and what Rose called the Earth Mother type. And Etta Chynoweth fell into the latter category. How strange that her life had evolved in such a way that she had had to live up to her name. Etta had once explained that it was of German origin and meant ruler of the home. 'Yes. Go on.'

'Well, this tall, good-looking guy came in and had a look around. I thought at first that he hadn't got a clue what he wanted so I asked if I could help. It was then he said he'd like one of the necklaces but instead of me carving the name on the blocks he wanted the actual letters carved out of the wood.

'I said I could do it. The name he wanted was Etta. He offered to pay in advance. Later I suspected that he'd waited until the shop was empty before asking, and that's why he'd been so busy looking around.'

'Did he collect it?'

'Yes, about three or four weeks ago.'

Around the time of Etta's birthday, Rose thought. For a man of his supposed wealth it was not an extravagant gift, but it was personal and he would have known Etta could not have explained away gold or diamonds. It had to be the same man. 'Can you remember his name?'

'Oh, yes, that's easy, because here's another coincidence. About an hour ago I heard on the local radio that his place has been burgled.'

At that point Rose had sat down on the arm of a

chair. Coincidence? She did not think so. Maddy was still speaking: she made herself listen.

'He and his wife had been on holiday and they weren't expected back until next week. From what little the news said I gather he's rolling in money. Art works of all descriptions went missing. No sum was announced but they said the value was probably somewhere in the region of seven figures if the collections remained intact.'

Seven figures? Did Etta have any idea just how rich the man was?

'What's he called?'

'Sorry. Didn't I say? Roger Hammond.'

Roger Hammond. The name meant nothing to Rose. 'Thanks, Maddy. Can I let you know another time about getting together? I really would like to meet Julie.'

'Of course. I can't wait to see her, Rose. I'm so excited. I mean, first the letter, then she followed it up with a telephone call and we made the arrangements. It's as if she can't wait either. I didn't expect her to come down for several weeks. I just hope I'm not a great disappointment.' In her excitement the tragedy in the Chynoweth household took second place.

'You won't be, Maddy. You couldn't possibly be. Take care, I'll speak to you soon . . .'

Arthur and Evelyn sat quietly while Rose related all this to Jack even though they had heard it once already.

'What do you think, Jack? Is there any way you can speak to him discreetly?'

His head was buzzing and he was thankful he had not taken the tablets or he'd have probably passed out on

Rose's kitchen floor. 'You know I can't promise you that. But the local police will have checked that he really was on holiday, that this wasn't some sort of insurance scam. And if so, then he can't have had anything to do with Joe's death either.'

'Why not? If Roger Hammond was not the man Sarah saw with Mark, maybe it was someone else he hired to do the job, ensuring he was safely out of the country when it happened.'

'You do like to dramatise, Rose. Look, if you want someone dead, if you hire a hit man, you don't get him to push the intended victim over a not very high cliff on the off chance he'll break his neck. If this Hammond has as much money as you say, he could afford to get the best where there'd be no mistakes. And, as you pointed out, where does the heroin come in?'

'I suppose you're right.' She looked away, disappointed. Her earlier animation in believing she'd got it all worked out had evaporated. But Jack could always manage to deflate her. 'What do you think, then?'

'I think it really is time you stopped meddling and let us get on with our work without wasting valuable manpower on looking for you.'

Rose bit hard on her lower lip. She was trying not to lose her temper in front of her parents. 'Well, thank you, Jack. I really thought what I've told you would be helpful. I'm sorry if I was wrong. I won't make the same mistake again.' She knew she sounded more petulant than angry.

Arthur glanced at his wife and raised his eyebrows. If

these two carried on like this in front of people, what on earth must they be like when they were on their own? No wonder the relationship had come to an end.

Jack bowed his head and shook it in despair. All he had wanted was for Rose to be safe. He had gone to look for her, got injured for his efforts and his reward was this. He sighed in resignation and wished he had ignored her message. There were times when he wished he'd never met her at all.

When he looked up Rose realised how ill he was. His mouth was pinched, his face grey with pain and there were more than the usual amount of lines fanning out around his eyes. She knew then that his anger with her was akin to that of a mother who smacked a child who had run into the road but who had avoided being hit by a car. He was relieved that she was safe but he did not know how to tell her so. 'Jack, shall I order you a taxi? It's eleven-thirty and you really do look dreadful.' She did not want to be alone with him in his vulnerable state, she might end up doing or saying something she would later regret.

He smiled ruefully. 'Thank you for that, and yes, please do. All I want is bed.' His leg had stiffened. Out of nowhere he heard his mother's voice: 'It'll get worse before it gets better.' He hoped this was one instance where she was wrong.

A taxi from Stone's, the local Newlyn firm, arrived within minutes. The driver, used to collecting Rose, tooted and sat with the engine idling down on the main road. Rose took Jack's arm and helped him down the drive. He grunted with pain.

'There has to be a drugs connection.'

166

'Oh?' Rose steadied him as best she could. He weighed almost twice as much as she did.

'That damn trawler.'

'Trawler?'

But Jack refused to elucidate. He had said too much already, that was the whisky talking. It was time he learnt to keep his mouth shut when Rose was around.

Arriving home for the second time that night he did not even pause to put on lights. Grateful he had no stairs to negotiate, he limped into the bedroom, pulled off his clothes and flung his ruined trousers over the back of a chair. Lying awkwardly in bed, he pulled the duvet up and closed his eyes. He could sleep as long as he wanted, he was not expected to go into work in the morning.

His dreams had a nightmare quality, but not disturbing enough to wake him. Throughout them ran the same theme, one which his subconscious dictated he take note of it was partly to do with Douggie and partly to do with Sarah.

When he woke it was daylight but far later than he had imagined because there was no sunlight streaming into the room to indicate it was already after nine. There was only the steady hiss of rain pounding the pavement. It seemed fitting that the day should start as gloomily as his waking thoughts.

Flinging back the duvet he tried to stand, cursing at the pain. He reached for his stick and hobbled to the kitchen to make some strong coffee. While the kettle boiled he swallowed two of the painkillers and prayed they would work quickly.

Later he would ring in and see what Mark Hurte had had to say for himself. If he had been that eager to talk the mystery surrounding Joe's death might be explained and they would know what the trawler was up to. Jack still found Douggie's involvement disturbing. He wondered if the man had been meant to overhear the conversation and then relate it to the police to create a diversion. Yet an arrest had been made. Were they meant to have arrested Mark whilst something else was taking place? Surely not. The chances of Mark being found had been thin. Douggie was many things, but he was not a liar.

There was, he realised, a more logical explanation. Perhaps, like himself, Douggie had partaken of more whisky than was good for him and had simply got it wrong. And then he recalled his dreams and all that Rose had told him and he knew what had been bothering him. Rose had said that Sarah knew about her mother's affair, in which case she might also have known that Hammond would be away. Now that was a very interesting point.

Maybe by the end of the day he would know the whole story.

CHAPTER ELEVEN

Radio Cornwall played quietly all day in the kitchen. From the time Etta was aware that Sarah might be in danger she had listened to every local news bulletin. What she most dreaded hearing was that the body of a teenage girl had been found. There had been such media announcements before; no name would be given out until the relatives had been informed. She had always shuddered, but how different it felt to be one of those waiting relatives. When she did hear some news which concerned her Etta was astounded, although it was nothing to do with Sarah. Roger Hammond and his wife had returned from a holiday a week sooner than anticipated, the broadcaster announced, to discover that their house had been burgled in their absence. Etta wondered whether the early return had any relevance to herself, if the time Roger had spent with his wife, Melanie, had been so unbearable that they'd decided to cut short their holiday and put an end to the marriage. She had no idea how she would feel if that was the case.

She was still thinking about this possibility half an hour

later when the telephone rang. Although it was rare for Roger to contact her by phone, Etta assumed it would be him, ringing for one of four reasons: to inform her of the burglary, to offer his condolences if he had heard about Joe, to say he was leaving Melanie or to call off their affair. It was not Roger.

'Mrs Chynoweth, we've found your daughter,' were the words she heard and had longed to hear for the past twenty-four hours. 'It's all right, she's perfectly well and unharmed.' The officer whose task it was to impart the good news had heard her gasp of pleasure and mistaken it for anxiety.

'Oh, thank you. Thank you. Where is she? Can I see her? When can she come home?' Etta's words tumbled out. She nodded as she listened. Sarah was being examined by a police surgeon, a precautionary measure only. Someone would bring her home immediately afterwards, but they needed to ask her some questions.

Etta felt light-headed and happier than she had been for days. She related the news to her parents and asked them if they would mind passing it on to her in-laws at their guest house whilst she went upstairs to wash her face and change. She wanted to look her best, and from now on Sarah would have a proper mother. For the first time in three days Etta applied some mascara and lipstick then waited for her daughter to come home.

She watched from the lounge window, waiting for the first glimpse of the car bringing Sarah back to her. It was still light but the air had a strange quality which Etta put down to her own emotions. A seagull squawked noisily on the roof of the house below as it walked sideways along its apex. As if it knew it was being observed it turned its head towards her, made a low, guttural sound, then flew off.

Everything seemed clearer and sharper now that she knew Sarah was safe. The glass in the window sparkled, the scent of the freesias in their vase on the table was stronger and her own body felt more alive, as if her circulation had speeded up. Cabbage white butterflies, their wings translucent, hovered over the nasturtiums which trailed over the edges of the raised borders. These would have emerged from their chrysalises in May, a second batch would hatch in August. These facts she had learnt from her father who, as a young man and in the days when it was fashionable, had collected butterflies. He had also told her that the French used to put eggshells in the garden, upon which the female would lay her eggs but upon which the young would starve. Was it true, or one of the stories with which he had entertained her? Tears filled her eyes. She brushed them away. It was ridiculous to feel nostalgic when the man she was thinking about was under her roof. In her expectant state Etta did not notice the dark clouds gathering on the horizon which promised rain.

It was another twenty minutes before one of the few cars using the road pulled up and stopped outside the gate at the side of the house. A car door slammed, then a second. Etta flung open the front door and ran out to meet her daughter.

Sarah stepped stiffly out of the back of the police car and fell into her mother's arms. 'I'm so sorry, Mum,' she sobbed. 'I'm so very sorry.'

Etta stroked her tangled hair. 'It's all right, love. It's all over now. You're home, that's the only thing that matters.'

The WPC and the detective sergeant who had accompanied her watched from a distance, allowing a few minutes for the tearful reunion. Etta seemed not to have noticed them. Releasing Sarah from her embrace, she took her hand and squeezed it. 'We'd better go inside,' she said, finally looking up and addressing the officers as she led the way past the clumps of thrift which spilt out onto the path. They ducked beneath the evergreen tamarisk tree with its feathery foliage. Ed had planted it as much for its resistance to salt winds as for its delicate flowers.

'We'll wait in the lounge,' her mother said a little tearfully after she had embraced Sarah and as Etta busied herself making tea, using those few minutes to say a silent thank you and gather her wits. 'Sarah won't want all of us listening to what she has to say.'

'Thanks, Mum. I'll bring your drinks in.'

Introductions were made. Etta was surprised at the informality. The WPC said her name was Jeanette and the detective sergeant said to call him Bob. He then explained that Sarah would have to make a proper statement in the morning, for now she was only required to answer a few straightforward questions.

She seemed bewildered. 'Can Mum stay?' It had already been explained to her that, at seventeen, she did not need the presence of a legal guardian when they questioned her. Jeanette indicated her agreement. 'I don't know where to start.'

'How about from the time Mark telephoned?' her mother suggested gently.

Sarah nodded and pushed back her hair with a thin hand. 'He asked me to go out with him on Sunday. I'd been seeing him for a couple of months, but not that often.' She risked a glance at Etta who smiled in encouragement and to show she was not angry.

'I met him as arranged and we drove to Zennor. I didn't know he'd got a car. We walked and talked – well, I did most of the talking. Mark seemed edgy. He doesn't usually like walking, I thought the outing was to please me. He bought me lunch in the pub but he didn't say much then either.

'Later, about four I think it was, he said he'd arranged to meet a friend but he wanted me to come too. He said his name was Terry.'

'Just Terry?' Bob asked as he made a note.

'Yes. We picked him up out by Safeway's and this Terry suggested we went to Porthleven. Mark drove round the roundabout and I thought that was where we were going. It wasn't, of course, we went to that hut. I only got suspicious when Mark turned off the main road, but it was too late by then. It was a two-door car and I was in the back. I couldn't get out.' She sounded agitated, as if the fear was more real now the ordeal was over.

'Take your time, Sarah. Have a break if you need it,' Bob told her.

'It's all right. I'm fine. They took me inside and locked the door. It was planned, I knew that by then, because there was a bag of groceries in the car and Terry carried them in with him. I thought Mark was my boyfriend. How could he do that to me? He was holding my arm; Terry had hold of the other one. There was no point in screaming, no one could possibly have heard me.' Sarah was twisting her hands. 'I'm sorry. It's just that now I'm home I keep thinking of all the things that could have happened.'

Etta stood up and went to her daughter. She hugged her, saddened by the dismay in her face and knowing she could not make amends for what had happened. Sarah had been betrayed by someone she thought had cared for her, and right on top of Joe's death.

'Mark said we had to stay there until Tuesday lunchtime then we could go home.'

'Tuesday lunchtime?' Bob frowned. Was that when the trawler was due to make its pick-up?

'I didn't believe him.' She paused, chewing her thumbnail, knowing that she might be in trouble if she now told the truth. 'I know I should've said something before, but on the night Joe died, I saw Mark and Terry on the road between Mousehole and Newlyn. I didn't know it was Terry then, of course. I was on the bus with Amy. She didn't see them and I didn't tell her I had done so. It was dark so the bus's inside lights were on. Mark turned around. He must've spotted me and told Terry who I was.'

There was a brief silence as this information was digested. Why hadn't Sarah come forward before? And why meet him at all if she thought she had anything to fear? They would leave it until tomorrow to find out.

'Did Mark know Joe?' It was Etta who asked. She leant forward, willing Sarah to keep on telling the truth.

'I'm not sure. By sight, yes, but I don't know if they ever spoke. Joe saw me with Mark once or twice.'

174

Etta sat back. How many more things had her children kept from her?

'I honestly can't think of any other reason why they were keeping me there other than my having seen them that night, but they didn't hurt me and they gave me food. Then I began to think that if I was right, if they'd been responsible for Joe's death, then they could never let me go as I could identify both of them.'

'Go on, Sarah,' Bob said. 'Anything else you can remember might be helpful.'

'Nothing really. They hardly spoke to me or to each other. Terry went out once for about an hour. Then, today, about four o'clock, I think it was, Terry said he had to go out again but he'd be back later. He handed something to Mark. It wasn't until later I realised it must've been the gun. I had no idea he was armed. Terry knew I couldn't escape with two of them there but he must've realised that I had far more chance with only Mark. Perhaps he thought I could even talk him into letting me go.

'The time went really slowly but Terry didn't come back and the next thing was we heard the police asking us to come out. I was so relieved. All I wanted was to come home. Then when Mark opened the door and fired a shot I couldn't believe it. I thought he was going to shoot me, too. After that – well, you know what happened.'

Bob nodded. 'Thank you, Sarah.' But what she had told them was of little help. They would never know if she would have been released in the morning or if Terry had intended returning, and if Mark Hurte didn't cough up they might never know why Sarah was held there at all. Terry had not taken the car, which had proved to be stolen. Had he returned as planned, he would have been on foot and therefore he would have had ample opportunity to see their cars and take off again without being seen himself.

'Was anyone hurt?' Etta asked. Her face was pale. She had had no idea a gun had been involved.

'Inspector Pearce sustained a flesh wound. It'll incapacitate him for a while, but he'll be okay.' It was the first time since she had introduced herself that the WPC had spoken. 'We'll leave it at that until the morning,' she continued, realising that the Chynoweth family had had enough for one day.

When they had gone Etta hugged Sarah again, holding her tightly, happier than words could express when she responded in kind. There would be no sleep for some time, not until she was sure Sarah really was all right and calm enough to be left on her own. 'Shall we have some more tea, and then I'll run you a bath?' Etta refilled the pot, her hands shaking with relief. When her own mother heard the front door close she popped her head around the kitchen door and said they were going to bed. 'We'll leave you two to talk. You can tell us all about it in the morning.'

'They were so worried,' Etta said when she heard her parents' slow footsteps on the landing above, 'but not as much as I was. It was awful, I was so scared I'd never see you again and we'd parted on not the best of terms. I just wanted you to know that I love you. I kept praying you could read my thoughts telepathically.' She touched Sarah's arm as if she needed reassurance she was really there.

'It was my fault, Mum,' Sarah bowed her head and

clasped her hands together to stop them from shaking. 'I was so angry with you I decided not to tell you about Mark. And then, when I saw him that night, I thought you might be right about my friends after all and I didn't want to admit that.' I might as well get it all over with, she thought, and began to explain to Etta how she had covered for Amy.

'Tell me, why were you so angry with me?' Etta spooned sugar into her cup. Her face felt hot, she was sure she knew what was coming, but it seemed a time for honesty and Etta would not shirk from the truth now that her daughter had provided such a good example. 'Was it because I disliked Amy and Roz?'

'No. It was because of that man you're seeing, I knew about it and I knew he was married. It seemed so unfair, you having a go at me about my friends when – well, when you were carrying on like that.'

'You're right. It was hypocritical. But it's over, Sarah. I won't be seeing him again.' It was a relief to have come to that decision. She would keep to her word whatever conclusions Roger had come to while he was in Greece. Nothing mattered more than the restoration of her remaining child. No, not a child, a woman, she realised. Nothing must come between them again. If she met another man, fine, but she would make sure he did not have a wife and he would not be hidden from Sarah. 'How did you know? You never said anything.'

'I was with Roz in St Ives. We saw you.'

Etta blushed and stared at her freckled, work-worn hands. 'I'm sorry. It was an awful way for you to find out.'

'He's very rich, isn't he?'

'You know him?'

Sarah shook her head. 'When he left you we followed him. He went up this long drive, it led to a big house with a swimming pool. We knew he lived there because he let himself in.'

Etta had never been there, had never even seen it. Her daughter knew something about Roger Hammond which she did not. She frowned. 'Did you or Roz ever mention this to anyone?'

'Why?'

'I just wondered. The house was broken into recently. It was on the news tonight. A lot of valuable things were taken, paintings mostly, I believe.'

'Oh, God.'

'Sarah? What is it?'

'I told Mark. I was so upset and Roz didn't seem to understand. She said good luck to you and that I should grow up because you were entitled to a life of your own. I thought Mark might take my side. He said he'd find out the man's name. It's Roger Hammond, isn't it?'

'Yes, Sarah, it is.' Roz may, as Etta suspected, be taking drugs, but she had far more common sense than she had credited her with if she believed adults were not over-the-hill once they reached forty.

'Oh, Mum, I think I've done something incredibly stupid.' Near to tears again, Sarah would not allow herself to cry. 'I also told Mark that Roger and his wife were going away.'

'But how on earth did you know that?' Feeling a need to do something with her hands other than clench and unclench them as she had been doing, Etta smoothed down her cotton dress and tucked her hair behind her ears.

'I overheard you on the phone. At first I wasn't sure it was him you were talking to, but when you hung up as soon as I came into the room I knew it couldn't be anyone else.'

Etta recalled the conversation which had taken place several days after she had met Roger that time in St Ives when they had snatched a few minutes together before he went away. 'We'll discuss it when you get back from Greece,' she had said, referring to their relationship. 'You've got a whole month to think about what I've said. Let's leave it in abeyance until then.' This is what Sarah must have heard.

'We'll have to tell the police.'

'But, Mum, if we do it'll all come out, about you and him. And what about his wife?'

'It's time we were both more honest with each other, Sarah. I promise you nothing like this will ever happen again. Anyway, it might not have to come out, and if it can be avoided I'd rather not hurt his wife.' Etta smiled wanly. 'Some boyfriend you picked if he is involved in the robbery as well.'

Sarah smiled back. 'You can talk.' It was the closest she had felt to her mother for a long time.

As they made their way upstairs the rain began to fall. Etta felt the prick of tears as it beat a tattoo on the attic skylight under which Joe had slept. She had not been up to his room since before his death. At some point she would have to face it, she would have to sort out his things. But with Sarah's help she thought she might be able to get through it.

* * *

179

Rose was standing in the kitchen doorway, a half smile on her face.

'You'll get wet, dear,' Evelyn said as she frowned at the low, grey sky. Rain was gusting into the kitchen, speckling the flagstone floor.

'I was just enjoying the fresh air. We needed this. And, believe it or not, I'd decided to water the garden today.'

Evelyn doubted that – it would have been left to Arthur who was far more particular about such things. 'Will it last, do you think? It was raining in the night.'

'Probably. Oh, did you hear that?' A distant rumble of thunder was just audible over the sounds of running water. 'If we're in for a summer storm it could last all day.'

'Then we'll have to find some way to amuse ourselves indoors, unless there's anything you'd like to see at the cinema.'

'Let's wait until Dad gets up before we decide.'

Arthur Forbes appeared minutes later. 'We're in for a storm,' he commented, missing the look which passed between mother and daughter.

'Yes, dear, we noticed.' Before she had finished speaking a flash of lightning lit up the bay which was then thrown back into relative darkness, the sun hidden behind a solid bank of charcoal cloud.

They took their coffee into the sitting room in order to be able to watch the storm. The sea was dark and menacing; white caps rose higher and higher as it rolled in towards the shore. Gulls shrieked and wheeled on their way inland to more sheltered places. The zigzags of lightning and claps of thunder came more frequently and what little daylight there was grew dimmer as the clouds took on even darker hues.

'It's quite exciting,' Evelyn said as the wind strengthened and howled around the house. All three stood in the recess of the bay window, steam from their drinks misting the glass. 'At least, from in here. I certainly wouldn't want to be out fishing in this.'

Over the noise of the elements Rose heard the telephone. It was Etta.

'Yes, I heard last night,' Rose said when she told her that Sarah was back. 'I was so pleased for you. I wanted to ring then but I guessed you wouldn't want to be disturbed.'

'The thing is, Rose, Sarah has some other information. It concerns what I was telling you. I don't think there's much chance of it remaining a secret any longer. Good heavens.'

They had both heard it and jumped. The storm was directly overhead now. Thunder seemed to shake the house and almost deafened them.

'You think I can help in some way?'

'I don't know, Rose. Oh, dear, I really hate doing this, it seems like taking advantage. Well, look, you couldn't tell Jack Pearce, could you? I mean now, before Sarah has to go and make her statement?'

'Etta, is this to do with the Hammond break-in?'

'Good heavens, yes. How did you know? Look, perhaps you'd like to have a word with Sarah.'

Before Rose could concur Sarah was already speaking. 'I told Mark that Mr Hammond would be away. I knew where he lived and that he was rich. It's all my fault, Rose, and now Mum's going to have to suffer for it.'

'Hang on, Sarah. You were with Mark from Sunday morning. We don't know when the burglary happened. You might actually be his alibi if it was after that time.'

'I know, but Mark wouldn't know how to get into somewhere that was alarmed, and a house like that must've been for insurance purposes.'

'I see what you mean. You think he used the information, or sold it, and someone else did the job?'

'Yes, something like that. Oh, God, what're the police going to think of me?'

'They might be annoyed that you didn't tell them about seeing Mark on that Thursday night before, but numerous people must've known that your mother's friend was rich. It wasn't a secret. What time do they want you to go in and make your statement?'

'About eleven.'

'Right. Then leave it with me. I'll speak to Jack and warn him – if he can make things easier for you, then I know he will.' Rose had her fingers crossed as she spoke. Jack would still be in bed if he had any sense. He needed rest and had obviously been in pain last night. The last thing he required was a begging phone call from her. 'I'll ring you back soon,' Rose promised, then turned to face her parents who had been unable to avoid hearing her side of the conversation.

'What now?' Evelyn asked, placing her coffee cup on the windowsill with a sigh of resignation.

'Nothing. I've just got to make a phone call.'

'To Jack? Honestly, that poor man. Can't you leave him in peace?'

'She never gave us any, my dear,' Arthur said. 'It makes a

change to see someone else on the receiving end.'

Rose took a deep breath and prepared herself for Jack's wrath. He took a long time to answer and she guessed he had had difficulty in getting out of bed and walking through the flat.

'Hello?'

'Hello, Jack. How're you feeling?'

'Christ! Did you ring at this ungodly hour just to ask me that? Like hell, if you must know.'

'I'm sorry.'

'Well?' he demanded after the several seconds of silence which followed.

'The thing is, Jack . . .' She heard his groan, ignored it and spoke quickly, telling him what Etta and Sarah had so recently told her.

'What on earth do you expect me to do about it? The girl's got to make a statement anyway. She can tell them herself.'

'She will, I'm sure. I was thinking more of Etta.'

'Ah, we're back to last night. You want me to cover up her affair, is that what you're asking?'

'I'm not asking anything. Etta wants to protect the wife, that's all.'

'Has it occurred to you that Mark Hurte might not be involved at all?'

'Yes. But it's also a possibility that he is.' I tried, Etta, Rose thought. Jack was in one of his stubborn moods, one where he would belittle or twist anything she said.

'Can I get back to you?' he asked, surprising her by his change of tack.

'Yes, of course. We'll be in all morning.'

'How is he?' Arthur inquired.

'The same as ever – bad-tempered and objectionable.'

'I meant his leg.'

Rose shrugged. 'It hurts, I expect.'

'Honestly, Rose, as far as I can see, you two deserve each other.' Evelyn had never witnessed her daughter interact with anyone in the way in which she did with Inspector Pearce.

Rose decided they would eat a proper breakfast and skip lunch. She lit the grill and got out hog's pudding, bacon, eggs, mushrooms and tomatoes. Cooking it would give her something to do until Jack returned her call. After she had heard from Jack she would get back to Etta.

'Smells delicious,' Arthur said appreciatively as the meat began to sizzle. 'Remind your mother to buy some hog's pudding to take home with us, won't you.' They both loved the loops of pale Cornish sausage which was sliced then grilled or fried. Each butcher had his own recipe and some added herbs to the filling. Their own butcher had laughed, thinking it a joke, when they had tried to purchase some after returning from their first visit to Rose and David's house soon after they were married. The Forbeses had had no idea then that it was only made in Cornwall and some areas of Devon.

They ate at the kitchen table with the lights on. There was no sign of the storm abating or the gloom dispelling. Rain lashed against the window, obscuring the view of the garden. Streams of water ran down the glass and the drain by the back door gurgled as the gutters overflowed and filled it.

Rose switched on the radio to listen to the news but it crackled so badly words were indecipherable. She swivelled the aerial but it made no difference so she gave up and sat down again. One day she would replace it with something more modern. But she had been telling herself that for years.

'Toast?' she asked when their plates were empty.

'Um, I wouldn't mind a slice.'

Evelyn declined and poked Arthur's waistline. 'You've already had a slice of fried bread.'

'I know, but you'll starve me when we get home, so allow me to enjoy my food whilst I can,' he told her.

'I don't starve you, Arthur, I try to give you a well-balanced diet.'

'Mum, could you see to it?' Rose indicated the grill under which a thick slice of crusty bread was beginning to turn golden, then she hurried to answer the telephone, hoping it was Jack and that he was ringing to say that everything would work out all right for Etta and Sarah Chynoweth.

CHAPTER TWELVE

Struggling to reach the telephone before the caller hung up, Jack surmised it could only be Rose who was ringing. 'Who else would be so damn inconsiderate?' he muttered as he half hopped across the room, trying to bear weight on the stick instead of his injured leg, but failing.

He had been awake for a while but had gone back to bed after drinking his coffee in the kitchen because he could not carry it without spilling it, not until he had mastered the dreaded walking stick. Lying in bed, on his good side, he had listened to the rain, knowing it was the best place to be, especially when thunder started crashing overhead. Now the blasted woman had disturbed him again. What chance did he have of healing quickly?

He heard Rose out with the intention of snubbing her, of telling her in no uncertain terms that he was not only off duty but recovering from flu and a gunshot wound and that his only plan for the day was complete rest. He might have added that she was thoughtless and selfish and a pain in the arse, although that would not have got him far. But as he listened an idea grew. Instead of cutting her off abruptly he found himself promising to get back to her.

Turning the hated stick upside-down, he used the crook end to drag a dining chair nearer to the phone. He sat down, his throbbing leg stretched out, which helped to ease the pain a little, then he dialled his own number at work and spoke to his counterpart who informed him that Mark Hurte had made a statement.

'Good. Can you give me the gist of it?' Jack listened carefully, making the occasional note on the pad he kept by the phone. 'Yes, well, keep trying,' he said. 'Any news on this trawler? It was supposed to land this morning. Blast it,' he said when he heard the answer. He tapped his teeth with the chewed end of a capless biro then shook his head in frustration. Every time they turned to follow new clues they only pointed in other directions. 'You're taking a statement from the Chynoweth girl this morning, I believe. This is what I'd like to ask her.' Jack explained what he wanted. 'And then go back to Hurte and see what he has to say about it.' His instructions were repeated back to him. 'Okay, that's it. Thanks. I'll be at home if there's anything new. Yes, I'll live,' he added in response to a belated question regarding his leg.

He replaced the receiver, thought for several seconds then rang Rose back. 'Fancy a coffee?' he asked sweetly, picturing her puzzled face, a pencil, no doubt, tucked behind her ear and the furrow on her forehead deepening in suspicion because she had no idea what he was up to. Well, good. She had kept him guessing often enough.

'Yes, if you're up to visitors.'

'I'm not really, it's just that I don't think I can make it to the kitchen so I thought I'd get you to come over and spoil me. How soon can you get here?'

'In about fifteen minutes. Jack, did you—'

'See you soon,' he said, cutting her off.

Jack wanted a long soak in the bath but it was an impossibility. He had been told not to get the dressings on his leg wet until he had seen his GP in two days' time. Which meant no shower either. Was there time to shave before Rose got there? He did not think so, it would take him that long to get to the bathroom. He rubbed a hand over the bristles on his chin and wondered just how bad he looked. There wasn't even a comb within reach. She would have to take him as he was. Perhaps he could persuade her to make the bed, not that a duvet needed much seeing to, but he hated leaving it in an untidy heap and he did not think he could balance long enough to give it a shake.

It was darker than ever. He reached out and pressed the switch on the table lamp but its low wattage bulb only threw out a small circle of light. Thunder continued to rumble, sometimes receding, distant for a few minutes, then returning again. Summer storms had a tendency to last for hours, as if they were at home in the bay and liked to make a day of it there.

Car tyres hissed and one or two pedestrians straggled past, bent beneath umbrellas which flapped in the wind. A car pulled in, headlamps on. The driver switched them off and cut the engine. It was Rose. He had not recognised the car because it was her parents'. They must have been parked behind her Metro and lent her theirs rather than get soaked moving it.

She ran to the door, her head unprotected, her hair flying about her face and shoulders. A sudden gust lifted it and she pulled her raincoat closer around her slender body.

'Damn it.' He had not thought to get up and start making his way to the door in preparation for her arrival. She would be saturated by the time he let her in.

The bell rang a second time and he called out, 'I'm on my way.'

Rose was bedraggled. She stepped over the threshold dripping water on to the black and white tiles of the hall floor. A droplet clung to the end of her nose then fell like a tear. The shoulders of her raincoat were soaked and her hair straggled around her face, darkened by the rain.

'You look a mess,' he said, with a wide grin.

'You might take a look in a mirror yourself, Inspector Pearce.' She squinted up at him. 'Did you really invite me over to make you coffee or is there something you wish to discuss?'

'Both. Coffee first. You wouldn't have abandoned your parents if you thought it was merely the former.'

Rose helped him back into the front room and settled him into a chair. She glanced around. Nothing had changed since her last visit. The grate in the marble surround fireplace stood empty. The flat was centrally heated, Jack never lit a fire, neither did he fill the large gaping fireplace with logs or dried flowers. There was a cobweb in the corner of the high ceiling but no dust on the mantelpiece or surfaces. Jack did his own housework and was not ashamed to admit it. He kept the flat reasonably clean and tidy but he had no desire to improve his surroundings. He considered the place as somewhere to sleep and, occasionally, to eat.

The three-piece suite and the carpet matched but the curtains did not. The furniture was old but not antique, although there were some nice pieces which were in keeping with the age and style of the building. Despite Jack's lack of interest it was a pleasant room which needed only a few touches to make it really attractive and welcoming. Rose knew better than to suggest so. She would have been told either to mind her own business or else to make the alterations herself, depending upon Jack's mood.

'Black or white?' He drank it both ways. She stood beside him noting his greyish pallor and the sheen of sweat on his brow. Unshaven, his hair still ruffled from sleep, he looked older but no less handsome.

'Black, please, two sugars. And there's a bottle of pills by the sink, can you bring them with you?'

He's in pain, she thought, far more than he'll let on. It was hard to imagine what being shot must have felt like, what would have gone through his mind when the bullet struck, if anything had at all. Maybe one day he'd tell her.

Rose made the coffee and carried the mugs across the hall into the front room. She placed them on the mats that were kept permanently on the table by the window and took a seat opposite Jack before sliding the plastic container of tablets towards him. 'They haven't given you many.'

'Enough to last until I see the doc on Thursday.'

They sipped their coffee, not entirely at ease in each other's company.

'Have you heard anything more about Joe?' Rose finally asked to break the silence in the room. Outside the rain continued to fall and the thunder to rumble. Gusts of wind rattled the sash windows. Rose could feel a draught from beneath the lower frame.

'I've been trying to work out what's going on here,' Jack began. 'These are the facts. Joe dies, a packet of heroin is found near his body, Sarah disappears only to be found with Mark Hurte who was seen with someone called Terry close to the place where Joe's body was found. Mark was armed. Sarah was told she was to be released on Tuesday, today, sometime after midday, but we don't know why that specific time was relevant or if it was true. Roger Hammond's house gets broken into, and Hammond just happens to be Etta Chynoweth's bit on the side.'

Rose flinched. It had not come across like that the way Etta had told her, but she let Jack continue uninterrupted.

'Out there is a trawler, anchored since the early hours of Monday and supposedly landing today.'

'Yes, you mentioned something about that last night. But why are you telling me now?'

Because it doesn't matter now, and because, for all I know, you just might have worked it out already, Rosie, dear – and if you have I want to know, he thought. 'Well, there has to be a connection. As far as I can make out, everything revolves around the Chynoweth family. On top of all that we were given information that a fishing boat might be trying to land something other than fish within the next few days. The day Tuesday in particular was mentioned.'

'Ah, the drugs connection.'

Jack shrugged. 'Possibly.'

'Well, as you know, Sarah happened to mention the relationship between her mother and Roger Hammond to Mark. I could make a good guess at some of it, Jack, but even knowing about the boat I can't get the drugs to fit in anywhere.' Rose gazed out of the window. It was almost a week since she'd done any work. She had a sudden desire to forget Jack Pearce and the Chynoweth family for a few hours and put on her oilskins and find a high spot where she could paint the broiling, storm-ridden sea, or walk in the rain with the wind in her face until she felt cleansed. But it wouldn't bring Joe back.

'Care to elucidate?'

'If you promise not to scoff.'

Jack raised his eyebrows and tried not to smile. Damp and dishevelled, wearing baggy jeans and a fisherman's shirt beneath the raincoat she had not bothered to remove, Rose still managed to look both provocative and fragile. He knew that the latter was far from the truth. He had made the mistake of thinking that before. 'Go on.'

'I think it was like this. Sarah met Mark and was either flattered by the attention of someone older, or she went out with him in defiance of Etta who disapproved of her friends. Not that they met on a regular basis, and then Sarah's friends told me Mark wasn't that interested, that he was probably using her. I also learnt something else.' She stopped. 'Look, Jack, there are things I'll tell you only if you promise not to act upon them.'

'Rose, be reasonable, you know I can't give you any such guarantee.'

She sighed. It was an unreasonable request. 'I know.'

She chewed her lip. Would it be a betrayal of Roz if she continued? Or would it be more a betrayal of Joe if she didn't? Perhaps she could word it in such a way that Roz need not be involved. She had liked the girl. No, too many lies had been told by other people, she would not add herself to the list. 'All right. Roz told me that Mark sells drugs. Nothing big, the odd joint, that kind of thing, but Sarah doesn't take them as far as I know.

'As you know, by chance Sarah and Roz discover that Etta is seeing Roger Hammond. They also discover, although not by chance, where he lives and that he's rich. Roz's view is that Etta's private life is her own concern and she doesn't show much sympathy for Sarah who is genuinely upset. Sarah, no doubt looking for comfort, confides all this to Mark. Mark, in turn, passes the information on; my guess is that it was Terry he told. No one seems to know anything about this Terry but it could be that he has friends in that line of business. I mean breaking and entering or whatever the legal terminology is. Meanwhile they've encountered Joe, for whatever reason, and he has to be silenced.'

'Why?' Jack leant forward, forgetting his leg, and flinched with pain. 'Why on earth would they need to silence him?' It was the big question, the answer to which eluded him. Could it have been an accident after all?

'I've thought a lot about this. There could be several reasons why they encountered each other. Maybe Mark told Joe about his mother's affair and he and Terry asked him to go in on the burglary job as a way of revenge on Hammond, maybe they wanted him to bring in something on the boat, or maybe Joe approached them with the intention of warning Mark to keep away from Sarah. He would have hated the idea of his sister being mixed up with someone involved with drugs.'

'You're not making much sense, Rose.'

'I know. It all seems clear in my head, I just can't explain it properly.'

'Have another go. I've got all day.'

'If Mark did pass on the information about Hammond and the fact that he would be away for some time, maybe the heroin was his payment. If there was a struggle perhaps the packet went over the side with Joe or maybe it was put there to draw attention away from what really took place that night. Sarah believes Mark saw her on that bus and that he told Terry she'd seen them, so they had to do something about it. As you said, you don't know if she would have been released today, but I think it's possible. They had taken her to a place where she was unlikely to be found so why not kill her immediately and make a run for it? Because, if they were involved in the break-in at the Hammond place, they wanted her out of the way only until the job was over and the stuff out of the county. Terry had already made his exit and Mark was left with Sarah, armed and holding the baby, so to speak.'

'Good point.'

'How did they find her, by the way? Or, rather, the hut?'

'Not by great detective work, as it happens. When you mentioned that she and Mark used a hut or shed as a place to meet we started a search of any likely building in the area. One of the officers on the case goes fishing in his spare time; a rod and line man. He'd seen the shed from his boat on several occasions.'

'I see.' She paused. Her information had been more than useful. She had yet to receive a thank you for it. 'Anyway, in the end I came to the conclusion that Sarah's disappearance was nothing to do with Joe's death. Roger Hammond wasn't expected home for another week. I think the burglary took place on Sunday and that's why they wanted Sarah out of the way. If someone discovered it the same day and Sarah heard about it on the news she might have gone straight to the police and admitted what she'd told Mark before they had a chance to get clear of the area.

'You see, they obviously knew what they were doing and they would have had to pack the stuff to prevent it becoming damaged. Such things take time.'

'They?'

'Whoever Mark and Terry passed the information on to. If you haven't found them yet it must have been carefully planned. They probably broke in and packed the stuff during Sunday night and hid it over Monday night. Once it was on its way out of the county this morning, it was safe for Sarah to go home in the early afternoon.

'Now, according to Sarah, Terry left the hut late on Monday afternoon saying he would return. I don't believe he meant to do that. I think he went to join whoever he was in with, leaving Mark with the gun and Sarah as his hostage. Mark was too frightened to disobey Terry even if he ended up taking all the blame. No one knows who this Terry is or where he comes from. He'd probably intended all along to rejoin his accomplices at that point.' She paused for breath and to take another sip of coffee. It was almost cold. 'I'd imagine Mark hadn't got a clue what was really going on and panicked when you lot appeared. Could I be right?'

'Quite possibly.'

'You're not saying anything, Jack. Haven't you got any views on this?'

'Not as many as you, it seems.'

'Oh, my God!'

'What is it?'

'Think about it, Jack. You've been worried about that trawler. Suppose it isn't bringing something in, but taking something out? Such as Roger Hammond's collections. I mean, they can hardly go by train, they'd be stopped easily enough, and the only other way out of the county is by road, and that has to be via the Tamar Bridge or the one at Gunnislake, and they're both easy places to put up a roadblock.'

'Private plane?'

Rose shrugged but when she looked up she saw Jack was grinning. 'You're right. The perfect way out is by boat, especially a private craft which doesn't have to register its movements.'

'Then the trawler . . . ?'

'Ah, there's the snag. It's on its way in now. The Joint Intelligence Cell has wasted an awful lot of time waiting for it to move but they couldn't risk boarding it until they knew what it was up to. In the end they had no need to. It turned out to be engine trouble. The engineer thought he could repair it himself without extra expense, but

197

he failed. He'd been working on it non-stop since they anchored. He had to give up and another vessel went to its aid early this morning, taking out a spare part. They'd started back for Newlyn as soon as they realised what was wrong, but they broke down altogether and didn't quite make it. The powers that be couldn't take a chance on questioning the owner of the vessel in case he was also involved.'

Rose sat upright. Her hands were clasped around her mug and her lips were pursed in concentration. 'I still believe a boat's involved.' She thought some more. 'What if that trawler was a decoy? What if the crew were paid just to act suspiciously even though they weren't doing anything illegal? How did you know about it anyway?'

How, indeed, Jack thought. Douggie told me, although he didn't give me much to go on. Maybe he'd been paid to inform the police to be on the lookout, and whilst they were watching incoming traffic, another vessel was leaving with its stolen cargo. He got to his feet and hopped across the room, causing Rose to hide a smile at his awkwardness.

'Who're you ringing?'

'Plymouth. I think you're right, I think they need to watch anyone leaving. If it isn't too late.' He passed on the information and came back to the table.

'You think I might be right?' Her eyes lit up.

'Very possibly.'

'Jack, I've had another thought.'

'Oh, please. Spare me. Look, go and fetch some more coffee like the good woman you are then tell me what else has crossed your clever little mind.'

'You didn't take your painkillers,' Rose pointed out, for once ignoring one of his more patronising remarks which would normally have brought forth a sharp retort.

'The rain's easing,' she said, when she returned with two more mugs of coffee. 'I saw a patch of blue from your kitchen window.'

'I'm not interested in the weather, Rose. Tell me what else you think.' This time he did pick up the container and, frowning, finally twisted off the childproof lid and swallowed two of the tablets.

'This comes back to Joe again. I'd thought of three reasons why he might have come into contact with Mark and Terry, which I've just given you, but supposing they asked him if he was prepared to take some boxes out to sea? The trawler would be empty on its outward voyage – well, apart from fuel and supplies – so there'd be plenty of room. It would be easy enough to sail so many miles out to sea and meet another boat who would relieve them of their cargo, then they could carry on fishing as normal and no one would be any the wiser.'

'The idea had crossed my mind, too, but it still comes back to the same thing: Joe was not the skipper, he would not have been able to make the decision.'

Rose sighed and pushed back her hair. It was beginning to dry, the waves kinking back into shape. 'So what happens now?'

'Both Sarah and Hurte are being interviewed this morning. Sarah will be asked questions and asked to make a statement in a far more formal setting than her home and without the presence of her mother, which wasn't strictly necessary last night.'

'Oh? But the nice, kind policeman realised she needed her mum?'

'We're not all the bastards you think we are, Rose.'

True, she thought, but two can play at that game. Repayment for earlier. We're quits again.

'We might hear a totally different version of events from the girl this morning, and at least we'll be able to compare what she and Hurte say. It's just a bloody nuisance we haven't got a lead on Terry.'

'But you will, if he's got a record.'

'Quite. *If* he's got a record. Without one any fingerprints found in that hut will be useless. We don't even know his surname, or if, indeed, he is called Terry.'

'Look, I'd better go, Jack. I don't want to worry my parents again, although they know I'm with you.' She laughed as she buttoned up her raincoat.

'What's so funny about that?'

'Nothing.' Rose shivered. The dampness had penetrated the lining of her mac. She was not about to repeat to Jack her father's parting shot or her mother's acid reply. 'Well, she ought to be safe enough there,' he'd said.

'Oh, she'll be all right, it's Jack I'm worried about, especially in his weakened state,' Evelyn had stated.

Rose had been wrong about the weather, the tiny patch of lighter sky had been swallowed up by cloud. She drove home through the dismal gloom, the windscreen wipers sending sheets of water left and right. She parked her father's car behind her own and opened the kitchen door. A wet and doleful-looking Laura was sitting at the table with her mother.

'You're soaked,' Evelyn said. 'Take that thing off and I'll hang it up.'

Rose took off her raincoat and handed it to her mother. 'Hi, Laura. Have they been entertaining you?'

'Filling me in on your latest exploits, more like it.'

'Not this time. I haven't done anything, it's Jack who had the lucky escape.'

'Mm. So I understand.'

'Where's Dad?' Rose asked.

'He's in the sitting room watching cricket with the sound down. It's not raining in London.'

'Oh, good.' They would not be interrupted. 'You're not your usual cheery little self. What's up?' Rose studied her friend's face. Laura was always able to look on the bright side, with one exception, and that was where Trevor was concerned. There were lines in the tight skin of her thin face and her hands were restless in her lap. She had obviously not been there long because her black hair in its usual disarray was still misted with rain.

'It's Trevor,' she admitted, as Rose had known she would.

'Another row?'

'Shall I leave, dear?' Evelyn asked Laura, then looked at Rose with the same question in her eyes.

'No, Evelyn, do stay. Maybe you could give me the benefit of your wisdom.'

Evelyn laughed and patted Laura's shoulder. 'I might be older than you, but it's no guarantee I'm any wiser.'

'No, but your marriage works.'

Rose decided a brandy was called for. She avoided making eye contact with her mother. If she wanted to drink brandy at eleven-thirty in the morning, there was nothing to stop her doing so, not even parental disapproval. But even as she poured it she was aware that she still felt very much her mother's daughter, that certain things never changed no matter what age you reached.

The first glass she handed to Laura who accepted it without surprise or complaint, thus confirming Evelyn's opinion of her daughter's strange drinking habits. But both girls, as she thought of them, seemed a bit down and they were both wet, maybe it wasn't such a bad idea after all. 'Don't I get one, too?' she asked with a smile.

'Of course.' Rose raised her eyebrows at Laura. 'Now, if you want my advice you'll have to tell me what Trevor's done to upset you.'

'Nothing, Evelyn, that's the point. Nothing I can put my finger on. I shouldn't have mentioned it, I really came to find out if Rose knew if there's any date set for the funeral yet.'

'No. But surely Trevor as one of the crew will be one of the first to be told,' Rose said.

'Yes, but he's not speaking to me.'

'Why not?'

'Oh, Rose, it's so ridiculous. It all started the other day as a bit of fun. He said he was thinking of giving up fishing. He could see I was horrified. It would never work, not if we were together all the time.

'He made a joke of it then, but he must have been thinking about my reaction, brooding, I suppose, you know, the way he does. Now he says I'm selfish, that I'm happy to live off his wages as long as I don't have to put up with him in the house.'

'Mm.' Evelyn had one finger to her lips. 'It could seem that way, I suppose. Have you tried to discuss it with him, to reassure him?'

'Trying to discuss anything with that man when he doesn't want to know is like fishing for crab in December.'

'Meaning it's a waste of time,' Rose added, in case her mother was not *au fait* with the patterns of marine life.

'But are you serious, Laura? Would you really not be able to cope if he got a job on land?' Evelyn could not understand it because she and Arthur had rarely spent a night apart. Maybe it was considered old-fashioned now, but they had been, and still were, unusually close, working in tandem when they had the farm. It had been easier for them than for some when Arthur retired, they were used to one another's daily company.

'Yes. I'm sure I'd get used to it eventually, but what Trevor won't see is that he's as much at fault as me. It's not as if he's even thinking about giving it up, but he's still got to make an issue of it.'

'Oh, come on, Laura. Think about it. Trevor would normally be going back out to sea, when?'

'Tomorrow.'

'Exactly. And Billy's said they won't do another trip until after Joe's funeral, right?'

Laura nodded, her cascade of curls bobbing around the neon pink of their restraining band.

'And there's no date yet for the funeral because the inquest isn't until tomorrow, and if Joe's body is released for burial, then the service still can't be arranged for at least another few days.'

'Oh, Rosie.' Laura jumped up and kissed her, long limbs flying everywhere. 'I should've realised what's eating him.'

'Rose?' Evelyn looked from one to the other.

'Despite what Trevor's told Laura, he's doing exactly what he always does, and Laura, his wife for more years than I care to remember, never sees it. His problem is that he can't wait to get back to sea.'

'I don't understand.'

'Many fishermen feel the same ambivalence. When he's out there he hates it and can't wait to land. Once he's been back for a couple of days he can't wait to go again. But this time he doesn't know when that's likely to be and he's restless.'

'Well, if you do want my advice, Laura, the old methods rarely fail.'

'Meaning what?'

'A nice meal, a few smiles, an apology, that sort of thing. What've I said?' She looked from Laura to Rose and back again. They were both laughing, doubled up, unable to stop. Laura was clutching her stomach. She did not know that they often found the same things funny and could still, even at their age, collapse, giggling like schoolgirls, tears running down their faces, nor did she know what she could possibly have said that was so funny. The astonishment on her own face made them laugh harder.

'Oh, Mum, you don't . . .' But Rose couldn't continue because she'd caught Laura's eye again.

'Oh, Evelyn. Never in a million years,' Laura added, her shoulders shaking as more laughter welled up.

'She's as feisty as you are, Rose,' Evelyn commented

with a sniff, disappointed her sensible advice had been so soundly rejected.

Her maternal instincts reasserted themselves when Laura started hiccupping. She went to the sink and poured her a glass of water then went to join Arthur where watching cricket would seem like the lesser of two evils.

CHAPTER THIRTEEN

Melanie Hammond stood behind the tall terrace windows and watched the rain bouncing off the broad leaves of the plants in her sub-tropical garden. The outlines of the plants were blurred by the snakes of water running down the glass but she was aware that the green stems of the fig with its nine-fingered leaves were no longer drooping. The roots drank greedily and the plant soon recovered from lack of water. If only she and Roger could recover so quickly.

They had called out an emergency repair man last night and the house had been made safe again but the feeling of violation remained, and she was not sure how much longer she could keep her secret.

Melanie had dressed in smartly creased summer-weight trousers with a narrow belt and a silk blouse. The belt felt tight. A knitted jacket was draped around her shoulders and on her feet were red Italian leather sandals. Everything she wore had been paid for by Roger. He had always treated her far better than she deserved.

A sudden gust of wind dashed more rain against the

window and made her jump. She felt cold, chilled from within, the weather was not responsible. The holiday had been good, had relaxed them both, but the homecoming had soured it. In half an hour the police would return and she and Roger would answer more of their questions, although whether they would be able to stick to the truth was doubtful. She was convinced that Roger was seeing another woman, he was bound to have told her he would be away, and there was her own past to consider. She had not thought about William Beddows in years but last night, unable to sleep, she had thought of nothing else. How much more trouble could she bring to Roger's door? She had to hope that she was wrong.

The world had turned upside-down. Melanie smiled wryly. In her experience, every good thing was always balanced by a bad one. She decided to wait until the police had been before she mentioned to Roger what she had known for a month, but only if she had guessed correctly, only if the circumstances were right.

The house was covered in fingerprint dust which she had felt disinclined to do anything about. Despite their wealth they did not have a cleaner or a gardener; Melanie preferred to see to things herself. As she no longer held down a job menial tasks kept her occupied and she had discovered that they did not, as she had imagined, either bore her or free her mind, but, instead, diverted her thoughts from the thing which caused her the most pain. She did not miss her job as a buyer for the accessories floor in a department store. When she left it to move to Cornwall she realised she had seen enough gloves and handbags to last her a lifetime. In retrospect, the work she had been doing had come to seem shallow; running a house did not.

Roger opened the door quietly. Most of his movements were understated, although he was not self-effacing. He watched his wife for several seconds, wishing he could read her mind. 'Are you all right, darling?'

Melanie turned to face him, her arms folded beneath her breasts. 'Yes, I'm fine, Roger. I hope this interview won't take long. I know it's silly, but they made me feel so guilty yesterday, as if I'd crept back and burgled the place myself.'

Roger kissed her forehead. Her face was brown and the lighter streaks of her hair had been bleached by the sun. 'They have to be sure. Such things have been known to happen. Melly, I – no, it's nothing, forget it.' He rubbed his eyes. They stung. He had not slept much last night but he had tried not to let his wife, sleepless beside him, know it. While the loss of his possessions had hurt, that could be dealt with: hurting Etta was a different matter, but it had to be done.

'Your paintings meant a lot to you, didn't they?'

Roger sighed. 'They did, and the porcelain, and they should not have done. People are more important than possessions. I'd started to forget that. They were . . .'

'A substitute,' she finished for him. 'I know. I understand.'

Roger was wearing a suit. The beige cloth showed off his tan and his lean body but worry and lack of sleep had aged him. His eyes were red-rimmed. Melanie waited. She saw that there was something he wished to say.

'Can I ask you something? Have there been . . .?' he finally began. 'Any men since we moved down here?'

He smiled then. 'We know each other better than we suppose. We're both capable of reading each other's thoughts. Have there?' he added more quietly.

'No, Roger. Not in four years.' Tears sprang into her eyes. 'It was so stupid of me, I really don't know why I was doing it. Damn it, of course I do. Can I ask you something?'

'Of course.'

But there was no time. A car swung in through the gate and pulled up in front of the house. The police had arrived. 'Do I offer them coffee?'

'Not if you don't want to.'

Melanie nodded. 'You let them in.'

Roger did so. She heard voices in the hall which grew louder as they approached. She turned to the door and smiled. Two men, she noted, but this would be considered a big crime down here.

'I've notified the insurance company,' Roger was saying, 'and they need the case number. We've also had the necessary repairs made and arranged for more security.' He raised his hands, palms uppermost. 'Yes, I know. Stable doors and all that. Please, sit down.'

Melanie remained standing in the window. Roger was nervous, he was talking too much and she thought she knew why. He had told someone they would be away.

The police did not stay long. The scene-of-crime officers had examined the whole house yesterday; the two detectives had only wanted to go over the same ground already covered, to see if Mr or Mrs Hammond had remembered anything relevant overnight, such as someone they might have mentioned their forthcoming holiday to or visitors to the house who might have guessed how much the collections were worth.

They were at the door when Melanie said, 'Wait.' This was, she decided, a day for honesty. They turned in unison. 'Roger, what about that man from – where was it? A village somewhere near Leicester?'

Roger frowned. 'Beddows. Not the place, the man's name,' he added, seeing the incomprehension on the faces of the officers. 'It's probably nothing, but he made me an offer for some of my paintings on more than one occasion. I refused. I didn't buy them as investments, I bought them because I enjoy looking at them. As a collection of art it isn't worth a fraction of what the real collectors own, just over a million at the last valuation, and it's taken me twenty years to accumulate it. But, yes, he was rather insistent at the time.' He blushed and glanced at Melanie who added nothing.

'Do you happen to know his full name and address, sir?'

'William Beddows, and he lives somewhere in Leicestershire. I can't be more specific than that, I'm afraid, but he shouldn't be hard to find, he's an extremely rich man. But I honestly don't believe he'd stoop to this, not when he can afford to buy more or less whatever he wants.'

'We'll check anyway. Thank you for your time.'

The rain had eased a little and the thunder which had woken Melanie early had rolled away across the narrow part of the peninsula several hours ago. She had become used to the vagaries of West Cornwall weather and knew that it might be raining in Penzance when St Ives was bathed in sunshine.

'Were you serious about Beddows?' Roger asked, after he had shown their visitors out.

'I'm not sure. I didn't like him, you know that, Roger.' How ironical it would be if the one time she had resisted temptation it had resulted in this.

'That doesn't mean he's a thief.'

'No. But he'd hardly have come down here himself anyway. I don't know, maybe it was just something to say, but he was extremely persistent.'

'Melanie, what is it you're not saying?'

'Nothing, Roger. Really. It wasn't what you think. Shall we have some coffee?' She went to make it in the large, luxuriously appointed kitchen which was a pleasure to cook in. What she wasn't saying, and never would, was that she had gone to a hotel room with Beddows but had not gone through with it in the end. At first he had tried to get her to persuade Roger to sell the coveted paintings to him; Roger had already refused. Later, when she wouldn't take off her clothes, he had become furious. The evening had culminated in Beddows slapping her. Melanie had not been able to return home until the redness in her face subsided. She thought at the time that she was being used, and she was, but later she realised it was more than that. Beddows had been persistent about more than the paintings and she had had a hard job persuading him she did not want to see him again. It had been many months before he stopped pestering her. He seemed to be obsessed with her, telephoning every time he knew Roger was out, sending flowers anonymously and following her to and from work. Beddows had wanted what Roger possessed, his wife and

212

his paintings, perhaps only because he could not have them. Melanie poured the rich, dark Colombian coffee into bone china cups more relieved than ever that she had not given into the man.

But those days were over. For some reason she had settled down once they had moved away from the place where she had been told it was unlikely that she would ever bear another child.

They sat on the cream leather sofa side by side. The sky lightened from slate grey to oyster; the rain was now no more than a fine drizzle.

'You wanted to ask me something – what was it?'

'I'm not sure that I should. I don't think I have a right to know.'

'Please, Melanie? Isn't it time we stopped deceiving each other?'

'Is that what you've been doing, Roger?' There was no hint of an accusation in her voice, she was not in a position to be making one.

Roger took a deep breath. 'Yes. I have been seeing someone for several months.'

'And you needed the holiday to decide whether or not to continue doing so?'

How well she knows me, he thought. 'Yes and no. Deep down I've always known there could be no one but you. I was looking for something I believed you could not give me and then I discovered I only wanted what you had to offer.'

'No matter how awful?'

Roger smiled. 'No matter how awful. Can you forgive me?'

'How can you ask that of me?' She placed her cup and saucer on the wood block floor and held him. 'We've both been such fools. Oh, Roger!' He deserved to know, however things turned out.

'What is it?' He pulled back, horrified. Melanie rarely cried, let alone sobbed as she was doing now. He stroked her hair, not knowing what else to do, and let her weep into his shoulder, dampening the thin material of his jacket.

When she looked up her face was streaked with mascara. It made her look vulnerable. 'I don't know how to tell you, I just don't know what this'll do to us now. Everything happens to us when it's too late.'

'What're you talking about?' His stomach muscles clenched. Had she, now that he had decided to end his affair, finally met someone she preferred to him, someone she loved? She began to laugh and he wondered if she was hysterical and if he might have to slap her.

'Nothing ever goes according to plan, does it? I'd guessed, you see, before we went away, that there was someone else. It was only then I began to realise I might lose you, that your patience might not be endless. It's true what I told you, there's been no one else since we moved, and unless you believe me, it's useless, there'll be a question mark hanging over us for ever. But you have my word on it, Roger.'

He nodded, believing her but fearful of what was coming next. 'Are you one hundred per cent certain you no longer want to see this other woman? I really have to know.'

'You, too, have my word on it.'

Melanie sniffed and blew her nose on a crumpled tissue

she found in her cardigan pocket. If Roger had decided to leave her she would not have said what she was about to say. There could be nothing worse than keeping a man only because he felt he should stay. 'Your collections have been stolen. You said they were a substitute. Well, perhaps you won't need any more substitutes.'

'What? Melanie?' He shook her by the elbows then stopped himself quickly. 'Melanie, are you telling me you're pregnant?'

'Yes.'

'Oh, God.' Tears filled his own eyes as his wife finished wiping hers away. 'But I thought it was too late, I thought with the menopause and everything?'

'So did I. Apparently it's not uncommon. In fact, it's quite a risky time, especially for women who've had a family and don't want any more children and think they're safe. Dr Adams told me that the change can last for years, as long as ten years, before there's no risk, and in my case, because I'd started it early and given up all hope, I'd relaxed. But Roger. I'm forty, he warned me there could be complications and a higher risk of an abnormal baby.'

'Yes.' He was still unable to take it in. No wonder Melanie had seemed different lately. 'But there're tests they can do these days, from quite early on.'

'I know. But I'm not prepared to take them. That's what I was so afraid of telling you. This is our second chance, our only other chance – I'm prepared to take it whatever the consequences. I will love this baby no matter who she or he is, whatever it turns out to be. Will you be able to love it unconditionally?'

'Yes.'

The storm outside had passed but the air between them was electric. Roger paced the room trying to take in what his wife had said. This was a second chance for both of them, their only chance. Whatever else he did in life he must not ruin it. He knew what he had to do and he would do it at once. 'I have to make a telephone call, Melanie. I think you know why.'

She nodded and watched him leave the room. She would never know for certain if he had intended ending his affair, only that he was about to do so now.

It was fifteen minutes before he returned, his expression grim.

Melanie spoke first, not wanting to hear the outcome of that telephone call. 'It's strange, isn't it? We're about to experience the one thing we've always hoped for and in return you've lost your paintings. As I've always said, one bad thing for every good one.'

'More than one, Melly. The woman I was seeing, her son was killed while we were away. He was a bright young man. She's devastated.' He paused. They had been so preoccupied with their own problems that they had not listened to the news. 'She blames herself, she feels it's a punishment. In a way, I do too.'

'Oh, Roger. How awful.' Melanie bit her lip. She was not the only one to lose a child and how much harder when you had watched one grow into an adult. She had always been the guilty party yet everyone else seemed to be suffering for her present happiness.

Roger read her thoughts. 'It's all right, she was prepared

for what I told her, I think we'd both come to the same decision before we went away, and no, I don't feel the need to keep on seeing her because of what's happened. My sympathy is worthless compared to what she's going through and she doesn't want the complication of an old relationship in the midst of her grief. Now, get your coat on, I'm taking you out to lunch to celebrate.'

Etta walked away from the telephone wondering at the power of the instrument. Within twenty-four hours she had received both good and bad news over the line. She paused in the lounge doorway, listening to the rain. The black clouds ought to have echoed her mood, but they didn't. She suddenly realised that hearing Roger say those words had come as a relief, it was better he had ended the affair than her, at least she knew she would not be hurting him. Her spirits lifted a little. Tomorrow there was the inquest to get through, then she would take each day as it came. Inspector Pearce had advised her as to the form the inquest would take.

'Mum?' Etta was smiling, properly smiling. Sarah had thought she might never do so again.

'That was Roger Hammond, Sarah. We won't be seeing each other again.'

Sarah hugged her but pulled away quickly. These recent displays of affection still embarrassed her. 'Aren't you sad?'

'Strangely enough, I'm not. Now, let's have some coffee.' No, she thought, I shall miss him for a while but that seems so insignificant when I think about losing Joe. And having Sarah back more than compensated for losing the few hours she and Roger had shared.

'I'll make it, you sit down.'

Etta did so, wondering why small kindnesses made her feel so raw and tearful. It'll pass, she told herself. Look at Rose, she got through it, as had Roger's wife many years ago. It was hard to accept that her daughter might be responsible for his recent financial loss but she was more to blame. If she had not met Roger it would not have happened.

Jack had manoeuvred an armchair to within reach of the phone and waited for it to ring. When it did he picked it up immediately and learnt that the statements given by Mark Hurte and Sarah Chynoweth differed on several points. 'Does Beddows fit the picture?' he asked when he heard what the Hammonds had said.

Indeed he does, he thought, because William Beddows owned a yacht.

He had told Rose he would get in touch later but had forgotten his promise and only remembered when Evelyn rang.

'Jack, my daughter's manners are atrocious. We can't have you hobbling around making do with a sandwich. I insist you come over for dinner. Arthur will collect you and drive you back, or Rose can.'

'Thank you, Mrs Forbes, but—'

'Evelyn, Jack. Don't go all formal on me.'

'All right. But what does Rose have to say about it?'

'She'll be delighted to see you. She's in the kitchen now, making lettuce soup and doing something with one of the ugliest fishes I've ever set eyes on. Now, six-thirty?'

We'll have time for a drink before dinner then.'

'If you're sure.'

'I'm quite sure. Goodbye, Jack.'

He hung up. That was the problem of food solved but his leg was not getting as much rest as it ought to have done. However, if the various cases were concluded by tonight, or tomorrow morning at the latest, he would feel no guilt in taking a whole week off.

He was disappointed when it was Arthur and not Rose who came to collect him, but grateful all the same for a change of scenery. It was a long time since he had been cooped up in the flat all day, and the weather added to his vague depression.

'She's pushing the boat out tonight,' Arthur said. 'It must be for your benefit,' he added with a barely concealed smile.

'I doubt that very much, Arthur. She just likes cooking, especially for those who appreciate food.'

'Ah, well.'

They continued the drive in silence. The storm had ended mid-afternoon and a watery sun spread pale fingers between the clouds. The roads were still wet but steaming in the warmth of what might turn out to be a nice evening. The sea was calmer but the tide was still running in fast. Ahead, in Newlyn harbour, the tall beams of the trawlers in their upright position could be seen. Not many, though – those that had gone to sea would have been way out beyond the storm and not in any danger.

Jack turned to Arthur when he indicated and pulled in

outside the Star Inn. 'Are we meeting them here?' he asked.

'No. I fancied a quick pint first – if you're up to it, that is?'

Jack levered himself out of the car. Either his leg was healing fast or he was becoming used to the pain. He suspected it was the latter.

The pub was busier than they had anticipated because trade depended largely upon how many boats were in. Jack knew many of the customers, they had been to school with him, and Arthur, through Rose, was on nodding acquaintance with some of them.

'What'll it be?'

'My shout,' Arthur insisted as he ordered two pints of bitter. 'Shall we sit or are you better off standing?'

'Standing, I think.'

They moved to the corner of the short end of the bar where no one needed to push past and there was less chance of Jack's leg being bumped accidentally. Jack waited. He was sure there was an ulterior motive for this unorchestrated part of the evening.

'How well do you know Rose, Jack?' Arthur looked ahead, as if the conversation was of no importance.

Jack considered the question before he answered it, watching the weather-beaten, angular profile of Rose's father. 'I'm never very sure. Just when I think I've got to the bottom of her, she surprises me. But then, I don't suppose anyone ever knows another person totally. Why do you ask?'

'I don't feel I know her either on occasions. Look, Jack,' Arthur turned to face him, 'this is probably too big a favour to ask, but would you sort of keep an eye on her?'

Even above the loud conversations Jack's laughter caused heads to turn. 'I think you're asking the impossible. She isn't one to be dictated to, nor will she take advice readily, but for your sake, I'll try.'

'You mean she's stubborn.'

'Yes, to put it mildly. Tell her one thing and she'll do the opposite.'

'Yes, I know.' Arthur sighed.

'But handled tactfully?' Jack grinned. 'Is that why we're here? You want to employ me as her bodyguard?'

'Put like that, it sounds rather ridiculous. I should not have asked you. Come on, we'd better drink up or we'll be in trouble.'

'Ah, there you are,' Evelyn said, smelling the beer. Her tone suggested that they were several hours late rather than twenty minutes.

'Hello, Jack.' Rose was peering into the oven. 'Help yourself to a drink.'

Evelyn tutted. 'I'll get it, Jack, you go in there and sit down.'

Satisfied that the food needed no more attention for a while, Rose joined them in the sitting room. 'You were going to ring me to let me know what happened today.'

'Yes. I was tied up.' It was safe to talk about it. Mark Hurte's arrest and the charges brought against him had been released to the media. 'A lot of what you said was right, Rose. And what's more, it's good news for Etta Chynoweth. Nothing can bring Joe back but, hard as it seems to believe, we now know his death was accidental.'

Rose leant forward, her glass clasped between both hands. Her eyes were shining in anticipation. Jack looked away. Her cleavage was visible in the V-neck of her pale green cotton dress. It made him uneasy, aware of her power over him. He was never sure if he preferred her hair up or down. Tonight it was loose and she had put on some make-up but she still gave the impression of being totally inaccessible.

'Accidental?'

'I'll start at the beginning. Hurte was made aware that Sarah had made a statement. In his second interview he was far more forthcoming but he claimed he hadn't seen Sarah on the bus that night.'

'Of course not. That was puzzling me. If he had done so and then told Terry, they would not have waited until Sunday to pick her up. She would already have had over two days in which to go to the police. Sorry, go on.'

'He met Beddows by chance and—'

'Beddows?'

Jack shook his head, forgetting that, for once, he was several steps ahead of Rose. 'Terry Beddows, the man he was with. Beddows had been sent down here by his father, a man named William Beddows. Now, the story goes back a long way. Beddows senior wanted two of the paintings possessed by Hammond. Terry was to find out where he lived, take a look at the security system then report back. His father would then send down the appropriate men to do the job.

'Luck was with him. When he came across Hurte, who knew the Chynoweth family and all about Etta's connection with Hammond, he got more information than he bargained for. It was a gift from the gods to discover exactly when the house would be unoccupied.'

'I said as much, didn't I? I thought it was more to do with the robbery than Joe's death.'

Arthur glanced at his wife and shook his head. His earlier request of Jack would prove fruitless, he saw that now, but he had asked at his wife's instigation.

'Quite. Terry Beddows was aware that if the break-in was discovered too soon Sarah might guess that Mark Hurte had been involved because she had been the one to pass on the relevant information. Beddows knew the plan, he also knew that he couldn't get away until Tuesday, so he persuaded Hurte that they needed to keep Sarah out of the way until then. The stuff was to be hidden for two nights to allow us to think it had already left the county if we happened to discover the burglary.'

'But what reason did he give Mark for wanting her out of the way until then?'

'He told him the truth, but he also told him that as the job was fixed for Sunday night Mark would have a perfect alibi. He would have been with Sarah the whole time. And he left him in no doubt as to what would happen to him if he didn't go along with it. This was the reason he was prepared to sit it out with Sarah until Tuesday lunchtime.'

'If you know all this you've obviously caught Terry Beddows.'

'Yes. Well, not me, of course. He and two other men set out in a launch late this morning. They weren't observed leaving shore so we suspect they must have hidden the craft in one of the small coves with the goods already aboard.

Anyway, there was, as we suspected, another boat waiting for them, not Beddows' father's yacht as we'd imagined, that would've been far too risky, but what looked like a rusty old tub. Our people in Plymouth had not given up watching and they were caught as they were transferring the crates on board. Hurte didn't confess to his knowledge of the robbery until he knew that Beddows was in custody. So, we got everyone who was involved, including William Beddows.'

'Don't look so smug, Jack. It was me who told you about the hut and the connection between Etta and Roger Hammond. If I hadn't found that out they might have got away with it.'

'You are, as always, quite right, Rose. Congratulations are in order.'

Arthur smiled to himself. Well done, Jack, he thought, tell her she's right, it takes the wind out of her sails.

'But how do you know Joe's death was an accident?'

'I was coming to that. He'd proposed to his girlfriend that night. She turned him down. We think he'd gone for a long walk, to cool off or think about life or whatever, but we'll never know for certain.

'He encountered Hurte and Beddows on that narrow bit of road near the old quarry where there's no pavement. There's no wooden fencing there either to protect pedestrians from the steep drop. According to Hurte, a car was drawing near on their side of the road and someone was approaching them on foot from the same direction; they didn't know it was Joe, and Beddows, not realising the danger, stepped out of the way. He slipped.

Joe grabbed his arm and Beddows struggled to keep his footing. In doing so Joe was thrown off balance and it was he who fell.'

'How awful,' Evelyn said. 'That young man lost his life trying to help a stranger.'

'And the heroin?' Rose asked.

'Hurte said that they made their way along to where there's safe access down to the shoreline. He was told to stay put while Beddows went down to see if Joe was all right. But Joe was dead. Hurte didn't know that at the time, he only heard it later on the radio and it was then he discovered the identity of the man. There hadn't been enough time for him to recognise Joe and there're no streetlights on that particular stretch of road.

'Apparently Beddows rejoined Hurte. He was smiling. He told Hurte that the man was winded but otherwise okay, that the bushes had broken his fall, and that he intended to make his way back along the lower level, which is quite possible. We can only assume he planted the heroin in order to confuse the issue, but he's not saying why he had it in the first place and I don't think he ever will. We came to the conclusion it was a little sideline of his.'

'Or, as I suggested, he intended using it to pay Mark off. Mark would have sold it and felt big. But what were they doing on that stretch of road in the first place?'

'Looking for a vehicle. Hurte told Beddows that cars were sometimes parked overnight in the lay-bys. They'd already decided it was too risky nicking one in Penzance, especially in view of the CCTV cameras.'

'What I don't understand is why Terry's father went to

so much trouble for a couple of paintings, and why take everything?'

'It's more complex than that. Or, the man himself is. It's all about obsession, Rose, obsession or maybe greed. William Beddows has always been just on the right side of the law. In other words, he's never been caught before. He's rich, but that isn't enough for him. He's acquisitive, but people and possessions only hold any value for him when they belong to someone else. I suppose when you have that much money, when you can afford anything you want, things to please you become harder to find. He was determined to have what Hammond had. Yes, it was only the two paintings he wanted but if nothing else was missing it would stand out a mile who had arranged for them to be taken.' Jack paused and looked at the three other occupants of the room. 'I take it this goes no further?'

'You have our word.' Arthur spoke for them all.

'It was an act of revenge as well. Melanie Hammond initially gave us Beddows' name, later she came in to make a voluntary statement. After he'd failed to persuade Hammond to sell he tried to get Melanie involved, promising anything she wanted in return for the paintings. He also tried to seduce her. In fact, for a long time he made a real nuisance of himself. Beddows not only wanted Hammond's pictures, he wanted his wife as well. It didn't seem to matter that he had one of his own.

'She was totally honest with us, she admitted to other affairs, but she said that Beddows revolted her, she had turned him down on both counts.'

'They can't have had a happy marriage, the Hammonds, not if they both had affairs.'

'No. But not everyone was as lucky as you, Rose.'

Evelyn was surprised at the forthright comment. Her daughter was on far more intimate terms with Jack Pearce than she had imagined if he was able to say such things to her.

Rose was quiet for a few minutes. She had been wrong, this was not about murder, but it was about a crime and, as Jack had pointed out, it all led back to the Chynoweths. 'It makes me sad. Joe's death was so unnecessary even if it was an accident. If neither party had been unfaithful Roger Hammond might not have been burgled, Mark and Terry might not have been on that particular piece of road and Joe would still be alive and Sarah would not have had to go through that ordeal.' She saw why Terry Beddows felt he had to leave Joe there: he could not afford to draw attention to himself and there was nothing he could have done for him. But it was an accident, she thought – he might at least have made an anonymous call from a phone box.

Jack coughed. 'Oh, yes.' Rose grinned, but she was blushing. 'And you might not have been shot.' She decided it was time to move on to happier things. 'I'll see to the rest of the meal,' she said as she stood up. 'Come and sit down in a couple of minutes.'

'She's some woman,' Jack said when she had left the room.

'Don't we know it.' Evelyn shook her head. 'And to think we only came down for a quiet week's holiday and the pleasure of being at her first solo exhibition. Oh, do look at that.' She was facing the bay. It had turned out to be a perfect summer's evening. The remnants of cloud had rolled inland leaving a clear blue sky. From the slightly open window came the pungent scents of damp soil and lavender. After the rain the air was fresher and the signs pointed to another fine day tomorrow.

'We've got one more full day, Arthur. Let's take Rose somewhere special.'

'Good idea. You can decide where.'

'Come on, it's ready.' Rose stood in the doorway, flowered oven gloves in her hand.

'Good. I'm hungry. And I can't wait to taste the fish.' Arthur said with what he hoped sounded like enthusiasm.

'Lettuce soup?' Jack whispered to him with a grimace as they followed Evelyn across the hall.

'I know. That's what I thought, but wait until you taste it. It's a lot nicer than it sounds. How's the leg bearing up?'

'Pretty well, really. Thanks for asking.' Which is more than your daughter has done, he thought. Then he smiled. In the kitchen he found Rose, just as he had known he would do, with a wine bottle between her knees as she tugged on the corkscrew.

No one mentioned the Chynoweths while they ate. The wine and food were delicious and the atmosphere lightened further when Rose described to Jack her mother's advice to Laura regarding her matrimonial problems.

'You really said that? To Laura? She's worse than Rose when it comes to taking advice. Can you imagine either of them pandering to a man?'

Rose scowled at him. Hadn't she just cooked him a meal?

'Worse than Rose? Impossible,' Arthur said, then decided he was on dangerous ground and concentrated on the strange-looking fish which had appeared on his plate.

Evelyn watched the interaction between Rose and Jack. Yes, she thought, Jack's feelings are obvious, how strange that Rose isn't aware of her own.

CHAPTER FOURTEEN

For the next couple of days the weather was unsettled until finally the thunderstorms cleared the air and gave way to scorching heat and summer proper.

Rose had not met Maddy's daughter. She had decided that it was too much to expect of Julie to make herself known to strangers as well as the mother she had never known over a two-day visit. She had also persuaded her parents to prolong their stay.

'In that case we'll all have a proper holiday, and no arguments, my girl,' Arthur had told her. He had wanted to take them to the Isles of Scilly but accommodation was at a premium in July and it was impossible to find anywhere with both a single and double room available. Instead, the day after Joe's funeral, they drove up to Devon, to the South Hams, and stayed at a farmhouse where they idled away the hours, soaking up sunshine in the garden while they read or taking long, leisurely walks on paths winding between ripened crops which were almost ready to harvest. There was a heavy summer stillness and the roughness of dried grasses rasped their legs as they walked. The hedgerows were filled with red campions, dog violets, bush vetch and stitchwort. The flowers of the brambles were interspersed with green and red berries, hard now, but they would be ready to pick in another month. Rose named those plants her parents did not know. She had drawn most of them for Barry's notelets. There were cream teas and strawberries and a bus ride to Bigbury where they crossed to Burgh Island in the sea-tractor and had cocktails in the 1920s art deco bar of the luxury hotel. The days passed quickly and they slept deeply at night, then suddenly it was over.

On the last afternoon Rose had taken her sketch pad out with her and her parents had watched in fascination as she quickly outlined the buccolic scene spread in front of them, then she drew the farmhouse and its garden, washing it in subtle watercolours before presenting it to Evelyn who hugged her in gratitude. 'In return for my jug,' Rose told her.

'She's itching to get back to work,' Evelyn said as they were getting ready for bed that night.

'I know, but the break's done her good. She needed it. I can't recall when she last had a holiday.'

'I won't hear of it,' Rose declared at breakfast when Arthur suggested they drove her home before setting off themselves. 'You'll almost double the length of your journey. Drop me at Plymouth station and I'll go back by train.'

They did so and Rose watched them drive away, sad at their going but knowing she was ready to get back to the routine of her life. She felt refreshed and was full of ideas for future work. Sitting on the train, her thoughts drifted from the holiday to Jack and to the events of the past few weeks and how fate, like most things, held a mixture of give and take.

Two people I know, two friends, and one has lost a son while the other has found a daughter. But Etta was a survivor. The sad day of the funeral had been and gone and now that she had Sarah on her side again it would be easier for her to get through the awful months which lay ahead. And Maddy, overjoyed that the child she had seen only briefly on that one sad occasion had come back to her, was now looking forward to a second visit.

The train neared Penzance. It slowed as the track took them through Marazion marshes. Rose saw St Michael's Mount rising out of the bay. Home, she thought, as she always did whenever it came into view. Feeling lazy she took a taxi home and opened the door to the thickness of stale heat. There was a mound of post and telephone messages to deal with and then a trip to the shops for food. It was after five before she had re-established herself.

Jack rang as she was pouring her pre-dinner wine. He was back at work, he said, and was just ringing to see if she had enjoyed herself and got home safely. 'And I wondered if you'd like to go out to eat? I don't suppose you've had a chance to do any shopping.'

'Not tonight, thanks, Jack. I'm ready for a night in.'

Another week passed before Geoff Carter renewed his

dinner invitation. Rose accepted it. They travelled to St Ives by train, the two carriages rattling along the line of the coast, miles of golden sand spread out way down below them. The azure sea was frilled with white foam as it rolled across the flat beach. They ate sea food and drank Chardonnay in glass goblets then returned home by taxi.

Over the scallops Rose learnt that Geoff was divorced, that his wife had left him for another man. He had been honest enough to admit that he had previously been unfaithful but had realised his mistake; an affair might seem exciting but living with the woman was not at all the same thing, and he had gone back to his wife.

'It was downhill from there,' he said as he poured more wine. 'I hadn't learnt my lesson, you see. When she found out for a second time, I was, quite rightly, shown the door.'

Rose had known immediately that things would progress no further, that even if Geoff had changed, which she doubted, she had gone past the stage of being prepared to be in a relationship where there could not be total trust. Geoff was handsome and relaxed and entertaining company but he lacked a sense of permanence. The Hammonds were a recent example of how much harm disloyalty could produce.

Each morning Rose left the house with her painting equipment in the back of the car or slung over her shoulder in her green canvas bag. She walked miles over rough ground, becoming fitter and browner each day. Where she worked depended upon her mood. Sometimes it was inland amongst rocky outcrops where the fern tips were already touched with brown and the lichen on the boulders was beginning to yellow. On other days she sat on a headland and tried to capture the colours of the sea, frustrating work as they changed so often, but now and then she sighed with pleasure, knowing she had got it just right.

One afternoon she sat on a cliff with the sun on her head and a gentle sea breeze blowing in her face and unscrewed her thermos flask. It contained the black coffee which sustained her whilst she was working. The steam rose and distorted her vision, making the horizon quiver. She lay on one side, ignoring the discomfort of the hard ground beneath her and the prickle of dry grass stalks through her skirt. Where is my life going? she wondered, thinking of the evening she had spent with Geoff Carter and the odd nights out she had with Jack.

Laura teased her, as Laura always did, but Rose had not returned Geoff's hospitality and had left the question of seeing him again unanswered. They would meet as friends or on a business footing, but no more than that.

'Anyway, you can bring him to my end of summer barbecue if you want. I've already invited Jack,' Laura had told her.

'That's typical of you. No one else I know would think of celebrating the end of something,' Rose had replied with a grin, ignoring her allusion to Geoff Carter. The discussion had taken place in the Swordfish bar during one of their companionable nights out. 'What if it's raining?'

'Then we'll go indoors. Live dangerously, that's what I say.' Laura had laid a hand on Rose's arm, her corkscrew curls bobbing as she laughed. 'Forget I said that, you're the last person to need encouragement.'

The night of the barbecue was not far off. Maddy's daughter, who was coming down again before the university term started, would be there. Rose was looking forward to meeting her. She had gone over to Maddy's for supper one evening and learnt that she and her daughter had found many things in common and had taken to each other at once. With great pride Maddy had shown Rose the photographs they had taken. The physical likeness between the two women was astonishing.

This isn't getting me anywhere, Rose thought, as she squinted through the long grass. Ants ran purposefully along the lengths of the stems and bees were busy amongst the heather. She found herself wondering which of them any daughter she and David might have produced would have favoured. A pointless conjecture, she decided, but without sadness or regret.

She sat up and looked around. There was no one in sight. For a while she had the world to herself, unless she counted the wildlife with whom she temporarily shared the headland. Her canvas was propped against a rock. She studied it for several minutes. It was good as far as it went, but there was something lacking. Without thinking she picked up a brush and began to work. It was a further two hours before she was satisfied and only the rumbling of her stomach dictated that it was time to go home.

She walked back to where she had parked the car and unlocked it. The trapped heat enveloped her as she opened the door. Make the most of it, she told herself, knowing that in a few short weeks things could be very different.

The coolness of the kitchen was welcome. Rose left the back door open while she unpacked her gear and the carrier of food she had purchased on her way home, including local strawberries which would soon be coming to an end.

Her face was hot and she hoped she had not overdone the sun although she had taken the precaution of wearing her battered straw hat. It was Jack's birthday in two days' time – ought she to buy him a present, and if so, what? It was difficult to find suitable gifts for men. I could just take him out or cook him a meal, I suppose, she thought, but I'll have to make sure he's not working that evening.

At six-thirty she opened her wine and prepared her food, drawing blood from a finger on a gurnard spike as she washed it. Once it was in the oven she went to the phone.

'Jack, are you busy on Thursday?'

'Why?'

Typical answer, she thought, find out what I want first. 'I thought I might treat you to a meal.'

'In that case, I'm not.'

'Here? Will that be all right?'

'You know I love your cooking, Rose. Thank you. I'll bring something suitable to wash it down with.'

'Wash it down?'

'Don't get teasy, you know what I mean.'

'No, I'll buy it. It is your birthday.'

'Thank you. I'll leave it to your impeccable taste then.' He had thought she would not remember it this year and had been careful not to mention it because he had not wanted to embarrass her. At the same time last year they had been a couple. He wished they still were. 'What time should I arrive and is it black tie?'

'Six-thirtyish, and wear what you like.'

Not long after this conversation Sarah arrived unannounced. 'These are for you,' she said, handing Rose a large box of chocolates, 'for all you've done.'

Rose was touched. 'Thank you.'

'And I felt I owed you an explanation. After what I told you, I mean. You must've thought I was crazy going out with Mark that day.'

'Yes, something like that. Fancy a glass of wine?'

'Please.' Sarah's face reflected her pleasure. It was great to be treated as an adult.

'Have a seat. Go on, then. Why did you?'

'I was sure no one would believe me, apart from you, that is, certainly not the police. I was hoping to trick him into an admission. I realised when he telephoned that he couldn't have seen me, he wouldn't have sounded so like himself. I really believed I wasn't in danger.'

'You weren't, not from that angle. And you couldn't have known about the Hammond break-in.'

Sarah blushed. 'But I was responsible for it.'

'No. A man from up country was responsible. It

would've happened sooner or later.' Rose switched the conversation to Sarah's career and later watched as she made her way down the drive. That she stopped to look at the view indicated to Rose that the girl was beginning to heal.

Two days later Jack appeared bearing a bunch of rather bedraggled flowers. 'I bought them this morning. I should've put them in water.' He kissed her cheek as he handed them to her.

'Thank you. But it's supposed to be your birthday.' Rose found a vase and arranged the wilting blossoms then went to the small room off the kitchen which had once been a larder but now housed the washing machine and freezer and several old pairs of shoes and coats. She had only thought of the champagne at the last minute and had put it in the freezer to chill. 'Now, here you are. A very happy birthday, Jack.' She handed him a flute in which the pale liquid fizzed and raised her own glass.

'My, my. Do I deserve this?' He grinned and raised his own glass in reply.

He was standing very close to her. Through the short-sleeved shirt he wore tucked into his jeans Rose felt the heat of his body. She smelt the crispness of freshly ironed cotton and his distinctive aftershave and moved away, wondering if it had been such a wise decision to invite him to dinner after all.

They sat outside enjoying the last of the day's sunshine. Jack's arm lay across the back of the seat but he did not allow his hand to drop to a position where his fingertips could rest on Rose's shoulder. 'How's Etta?' he asked.

'It's hard to say. Good days and bad.'

Jack nodded. 'And Sarah?'

'Almost human, Etta says.' Rose knew that Sarah had come to the adult decision not to socialise with Amy and Roz any more. She would, as planned, stay on at school. Etta had no immediate plans, which Rose agreed was sensible. 'I'm not ready to face the future yet,' she had told Rose over coffee one morning. 'I'm still taking life one day at a time.'

'It's the only way, but it works.' Rose said. She had mentioned Laura's barbecue knowing that, had Joe been alive, he would certainly have been invited. 'Are you and Sarah going?'

'I think so. I know Sarah will. I never know how I'm going to feel when I wake in the mornings. Laura just said to turn up if it was a good day.'

'It might do her good if she does go,' Jack said when Rose had related the conversation.

'It's still early days, Jack, she might feel disloyal.' Jack frowned. 'I know, it's daft. But after David died, after about a year, I suppose, I felt guilty if I felt the slightest happiness even though he would have wanted it for me.'

'I think I understand.' Jack reached beneath the bench but the champagne bottle they had placed there to keep cool was already empty. Their conversation had been easy, comfortable, that of old friends, and they had hardly noticed how much time had already passed. The nights were pulling in and a few stars glittered in the growing dusk. A half moon hung at an angle over the bay and a cricket chirruped somewhere near the shed. Rose had cleared it out, throwing away years of accumulated rubbish, and it had become another place where she could work.

'Are you ready to eat?' They stood up and went inside.

'You don't know how much I appreciate this,' Jack said as he picked up his knife to spread home-made crab pate on crusty bread. Conversation seemed unnecessary as they ate the meal Rose had taken such trouble in preparing.

When they had finished they drank coffee and brandy in the sitting room. Music played quietly in the background.

'Jack, that day when you found Sarah and were shot at, did you get into trouble over it?' He had given Rose an abridged version of what had happened that evening, but it was enough for her to guess that he had acted out of character, prompted by his belief that she had been with Mark and Sarah.

'Yes, but not as much as I could have done. Fortunately, I was the only injured party. I was very lucky to get off with a warning.' And he had been, he knew that. There could have been a disciplinary hearing, he might even have been demoted. He paused. 'You know that I thought you were in there, Rose. I would never have acted in that way otherwise.'

'Yes, you did tell me.' There seemed nothing more she could say. Rose bit her lip, unsure how she would respond if he became more intimate. She was curled in an armchair, her legs tucked beneath her. Any movement would have broken the mood they had created.

It was dark now, but she had not turned on the table lamps. Across the bay the lights of Marazion twinkled, echoed by the stars overhead. Jack's shape loomed over Rose without her having been aware he had risen. He reached out a hand, tilted her face up and kissed her on the lips. 'I've been wanting to do that for a very long time, Mrs Trevelyan.'

She froze, her emotions in conflict. She wanted him to go but she wanted him to stay. It had been hard not to respond. The next move was hers.

Jack waited, knowing what was going through her mind. She had come to a decision. She stood up slowly and took his hand. 'Well, it *is* your birthday.' Her smile turned into a frown. 'What is it, Jack? What've I said?'

'You really are a bitch sometimes, Rose.'

Pale-faced, she took a step backwards. 'Jack? I don't understand.'

'It was a lovely meal, a really special meal, thank you, but it's time I went home now.'

'You can't just walk off like that – what've I done now to make you angry?'

'You made it sound as if you were doing me a favour just because this happens to be a celebration of the day I was born.'

'Oh, honestly, how sensitive can you get? It was a joke, Jack, you know, something to do with a sense of humour, something you obviously don't possess.'

'Then why now, after all these months? You laid down the ground rules; friendship, you said, nothing more. And until tonight you've stuck by it, and so have I, as

242

difficult as it's been. Why the sudden volte-face?'

'Well, you started it by kissing me.' But what he said was true. Damn the champagne. It had been a bad idea to invite him. And what if they had gone upstairs and spent the night together, what then? What would he have expected afterwards? She had it in her power to hurt Jack again and she did not want to do that, nor did she want to lose his friendship. 'I'm sorry. You're right, I behaved foolishly. You'd better go now.'

He turned away. Too much champagne had been his downfall, too. What he had intended to say had come out wrong. He'd had his chance and he'd blown it. In fact, he should not have made a move at all.

'Do you want me to ring for a taxi?'

'No, thanks, I'll walk.'

She showed him to the kitchen door. The unwashed dishes mocked her; the evening had turned into a disaster. Neither of them now knew what to say, it was a complete contrast to how things had been earlier.

'Goodnight, Jack.' Rose was furious; with herself for ruining his birthday and with him for reacting as he had done. She grabbed a bottle of wine from the rack. Well, bugger him then, she'd have another drink then she would be able to sleep without reliving it all in her head and feeling guilty.

'The answer to everything, I see.' Jack nodded towards the bottle in her hand.

'No, Jack, not everything, just the answer to my stupidity tonight.'

'Are you really going to open it?'

243

'Yes.'

'Is that wise, after a bottle of champagne each?'

'Jack, this is my house, this is my wine which I paid for and my wisdom or otherwise does not concern you. Are you leaving or are you going to stand in the damn doorway all night?'

'Neither, not if you'd prefer to share that bottle. I ought to go home, but I don't like to think of you drinking alone, you know, getting maudlin and ringing me up in the middle of the night to apologise.'

'You know perfectly well I'd never . . .' But he was laughing, then so was Rose. 'Oh, sod you, Jack Pearce. Find yourself a glass then.'

As Rose flounced around the kitchen filling the kettle noisily and clattering the grill-pan, Jack's lips formed a thin, straight line but he could not disguise the laughter in his eyes. Rose might be regretting what had taken place but she could not alter it. 'You don't have to make me toast, I can easily get something on my way to work,' he said. 'I'll have to go home and change anyway.'

'Jack, I—' Rose kept her back to him, busy spreading butter.

'Don't say it, Rose. Whatever it is I'd rather not hear it. We can pretend last night never happened and carry on as before.' The smile had faded. Rose might have decided it was better if they did not see one another again.

'Thank you. I appreciate that.' She turned slowly, not sure what she would read in his face.

Jack nodded. 'Look, don't bother with that. I'm not

really hungry anyway. I'll give you a ring sometime, okay?'

'Okay.'

It was still early, only a little after seven, but Jack had to get back to the flat to change for work and collect his car. Rose watched him go from the kitchen door. He walked fast and turned left at the bottom of the drive without looking back. She sighed. The toast had gone cold but she was no longer hungry either.

Action was needed. Upstairs she stripped the bed although the sheets had been changed two days previously. But she did not want to smell Jack's aftershave on the pillow when she went to bed that night.

During the morning the weather changed. Like her feelings it became unsettled. Banks of cloud were swept across the bay, out towards the sea. Occasionally patches of blue sky were revealed only to disappear again. It was not cold but Rose shivered. She drank coffee and toyed with a sketch pad as the washing machine ran through its cycle. You shouldn't have done it, were the words which repeated themselves in her mind, you shouldn't have led him on.

The sheets flapped on the line, snapping and crackling in gusts of salty wind. Rose didn't care if it rained. Work was out of the question, her mood was all wrong. But there was something she could do. She picked up the parcel she had wrapped, then hesitated. Was it too soon? Would there ever be a right time?

The wind came at her sideways as she walked down the hill into Newlyn. When it dropped Rose could feel the sun on her head and the warmth rise from the pavement. Her pace increased and she knew she had been right to get out of the house.

The emerald sea was white-capped, the gulls mirroring its surface as they skimmed across the bay. It was a good day for walking. Striding along the length of the Promenade Rose began to feel better. She reached the Jubilee Pool and stopped to watch the swimmers before retracing her steps. At Wherrytown she crossed the road and walked up the hill to Etta's house. She and Sarah were both working in the back garden, taking advantage of a cooler day to pull out weeds. Something had altered between the two females, Rose sensed they had become friends.

'Come in, Rose,' Etta said. 'We were just going to make some coffee and it's time to stop or we'll both ache tomorrow.'

Through the open kitchen door which led to the hall Rose saw several bulging bin liners and realised what Etta and Sarah had been doing. Maybe this is the perfect time, she thought. The material accompaniments to Joe's life were about to be disposed of; what Rose had brought was the opposite, it was the embodiment of Joe himself. 'I'd like you to have this, but only if you want it,' Rose said, once the coffee was on the table.

'For me?' Etta took the rectangular package and peeled off the wrapping. She gasped. 'Oh, Rose, I don't know what to say. It's beautiful. Thank you.' Her eyes sparkled with a mixture of pleasure and unshed tears. She held the painting away from her. In the distance were the craggy cliffs of the Cornish coastline, in front was the open sea, neither calm nor rough, and slightly to the right, trailing wake and gathering a flock of gulls, was Billy Cadogan's trawler, the number on its port side clearly visible as it returned to harbour. The swarthy figure at the stern was indistinguishable, apart from his black hair. 'It's Billy's boat, and Joe, isn't it?' Etta said, her eyes still overbright.

'Yes. It's Joe.'

'It's really lovely, Rose.' Sarah took the oil from her mother and examined it closely. 'Over the fireplace?' she suggested.

'Yes. Over the fireplace where we'll always be able to see it.'

Rose had known subconsciously the day she had painted that scene that it had been destined for somewhere other than a gallery: in the back of her mind she had known what she must do for Etta and Sarah. It was when she had realised that something vital was missing that she had added the trawler and the figure who might have been anyone until she had painted in the registration number.

With the wind swirling her hair in all directions, Rose made her way home. Jack Pearce, for the moment, was forgotten.

Laura rang to invite her for supper. Trevor was at sea. Their argument had been resolved as soon as Billy said they were sailing when Laura and Trevor relaxed, both in need of the space about to be granted them.

'Drink? Silly question,' Laura said when Rose arrived. 'Red or white?'

'Either.'

'The wind's getting stronger.' Laura frowned. Once Trevor was out of her sight she worried about him. 'Is something wrong?' She looked at Rose carefully.

'No. I was thinking about how small my problems are compared with Sarah's. Not only has she lost her brother, she believed Mark was her boyfriend and look what he did to her. And he was partially responsible for Joe's death. It's a double betrayal.'

Laura knew all that had happened, and Billy had found a replacement for Joe. Life had to go on. 'It's more than that. You can't fool me, Rose. Which was it, late night or too much vino? Or both?'

Rose lowered her head but it was too late. Laura had seen the blush creeping up from her neck. 'Aha.' She tossed the mass of her hair back over her shoulders and sat down next to Rose, her thin legs encased in leggings stretched out in front of her. 'Might our debonair gallery owner have anything to do with this?' She tapped a finger to the side of her nose.

'Certainly not.'

'Certainly not,' Laura mimicked. 'Okay. Then there's only one person I can think of who makes you so indignant and prickly and that's Jack Pearce. I'm right, aren't I? You did the dirty deed, didn't you? Poor old Jack.'

'What do you mean, poor old Jack?'

Laura's grin widened and the lines in her almost skeletal face deepened as she pointed a long finger at Rose. 'See what I mean? God, everyone can see how he feels about you, why don't you admit what you feel about him?'

'I can't. I don't know. Oh, Laura, I'm not prepared to share my life to that extent.'

'Can't, or won't admit what you feel? Sometimes I think you need a good shake.' Laura turned her attention to the squid she was marinating.

'Can't,' Rose said with emphasis. 'You're right. I don't want to admit what I feel. Anyway, there's no harm in keeping my options open.'

'For what?' Laura turned to face her, the spatula in her hand dripping oil on the floor. 'Geoff Carter? Barry Rowe? Come off it, Rose.'

'No, not for them.' Rose smiled. 'For the future, for whatever it might hold for me.'

Laura shook her head. 'Anyone would think you were seventeen.' She had always hoped Rose and Jack would become a couple. 'You can be quite selfish at times, Rose. You want Jack only when you want him, at other times you keep him at a distance.'

'You can talk.'

'Meaning what?' Laura folded her arms, a fierce expression on her face, the spatula dripping further oil on to the floor.

'Meaning that little tiff you had with Trevor about him getting a land-based job?'

'Oh, that.' Laura grinned. 'Yeah, well, I get your point. It doesn't do to have them around all the time.'

'I'm starving, Mrs Penfold, do you think you could get a move on?' Rose returned Laura's smile. Yes, she did

249

still feel she was seventeen and that the future stretched ahead of her. Well, she would follow her advice to Etta and take one day at a time. For now there was her new career. And, of course, there was Laura's barbecue. And Jack would be there.

Rose Trevelyan had only met Gabrielle Milton once, but felt they might become good friends. She was delighted, therefore, to receive an invitation to the Milton's party where the wine flowed freely and a good time was being had by all - that is, until Gabrielle's crumpled, lifeless body was found underneath a balcony.

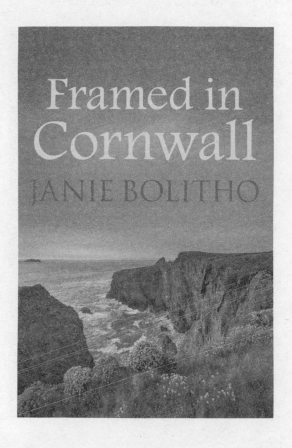

Dorothy Pengelly lived alone in her remote, dilapidated cottage with only her pets as company. When her old friend, Rose Trevelyan calls round to visit and finds Dorothy dead she is devastated. And when Rose learns that it wasn't a heart attack but a case of suicide her suspicions are immediately roused. Dorothy would never have killed herself – but would anyone have the motive to murder her?

To discover more great books and to
place an order visit our website at
allisonandbusby.com

Don't forget to sign up to our free newsletter at
allisonandbusby.com/newsletter
for latest releases, events and exclusive offers

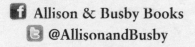 Allison & Busby Books
@AllisonandBusby

You can also call us on
020 7580 1080
for orders, queries
and reading recommendations